WANTING THE WINGER

LOVE ON THE LINE
BOOK TWO

BRENDA ROTHERT

CHAPTER ONE

Bash

"Damn, bro. The resemblance between you and your son is uncanny."

My teammate Carter cuts a glare at me. "Stop calling Darling my son."

I can't help smirking as I check out the photo he just showed me after we finished a six-mile run. Even though it's August, his wife Suki already had family photos done for their holiday cards this year, and they include the family pet, a pig named Darling.

"The girls call him their brother and Suki calls him her son. Why you gotta be so cold?"

"He's a two-hundred-and-eighty-two-pound pig and he ate one of my hockey sticks the other day. He's lucky I even let him live in the house."

Our teammate Leo shoves his shoulder. "I know you're not fat-shaming my nephew. I'll fucking fight you."

Carter shrugs and pulls off his sweat-soaked T-shirt. "You're both uninvited from fondue night."

"The fuck we are," I say. "Let me ask your boss about that."

Harry, one of Suki's best friends, is a chef. Once a month, he helps Suki host a fondue party for their family and close friends. It always has a huge spread of perfectly seasoned and cooked steak, chicken, vegetables and potatoes for the cheese fondue and assorted fruits and sweets for the chocolate fondue. It's my favorite meal of every month.

"Remind my boss who really wears the pants in our relationship," Carter says lightly. "I'm the man and I make the rules."

I scoff and reach for my phone. "I'll let her know."

He frowns. "No, don't."

"That's what I thought." I glance at my phone screen, finding messages waiting.

One is from Jana, who delivers my groceries.

Jana: They didn't have broccolini but they had broc-

coli so I got that. And they didn't have Junior Mints so I got mint M&Ms.

I roll my eyes and thumbs-up her message. It's fine on the broccoli, but not the candy. I'll have to stop on my way home later to find Junior Mints for my new roommate.

She's the one who sent the other message waiting for me.

Lainey: Running late. Can't fit everything in my car so I'm unpacking and trying again. It's not as fun as Tetris.

My jaw tenses. Why the fuck isn't Shane, her fiancé, packing his car up with her shit and driving her here?

Because he's a piece of shit. I already knew that, but I seem to be the only one. Lainey was cozied up to his side during their engagement party two months ago in Columbus, my hometown. And her brother Eric, who's been one of my best friends since we were kids, thinks Shane's good enough for his sister.

Not even close. When Lainey, who recently finished her master's degree in microbiology, got a chance to do a semester-long research project with a professor at Cleveland State University, I told her she was staying with me. The house I bought after signing with the Cleveland Comets three years ago has five bedrooms, so I have plenty of room for her.

And this will give me a chance to convince her to dump Shane's ass. She's only twenty-four—way too young to be getting married.

If her own brother won't talk some sense into her, I will. I've known her since she was a kindergartener with bright-red pigtails, and I'm not letting her make the biggest mistake of her life. I don't have to report to training camp for another month, so I've got lots of free time.

Carter pats my belly. "You're looking better than you were before last season started, Fatman."

"I look fucking great, douchebag. And I did last year, too."

That's not entirely true. I have a distinctive voice —it's deep and gravelly. Since high school, people have gotten a kick out of asking me to say, "I'm Batman" because I've got the voice for it. Knowing that, when I picked up fifteen pounds in the last offseason from slacking on my workouts and hiring an Italian chef, they hung up pictures of a heavyset cartoon Batman all over the locker room. And not just our locker room—visiting ones, too. Every time I walked into a room, they'd say, "I'm Fatman."

So I lost the weight and the joke died—mostly. I

didn't drop the pounds for those fuckers, though, but because I was so much slower. I can't let myself get out of shape again. Me, Leo and Carter have been running five days a week and lifting with our team trainers this offseason.

"Those are abs, by the way," I tell Carter. "You probably don't remember having those since you're a lazy married guy now."

A wrinkle forms between his brows as he looks down at his stomach. "I still have abs."

"Those are called *flabs*."

I take off my T-shirt, pointing at my own well-defined eight-pack. I've been on a high-protein Mediterranean diet for ten months now, and I'm in better shape than ever. The Fatman shit was a wake-up call. I have to stay in great shape, or I'm risking my career.

Carter shrugs. "I'll be back there when the season starts. Olivia has been doing a lot of baking and I can't not eat it."

"I get that."

Olivia is the oldest of his three nieces that he and Suki are raising. Their overdue honeymoon was at the start of our offseason in Hawaii and a bunch of us went with them to help with the kids.

"We're grilling out this evening. You guys want to come over?" Carter asks.

Leo scowls. "Will Mara be there?"

"She's Suki's best friend, what do you think?"

Leo lets out a humorless laugh. "Well, since you asked, I think she's an overly opinionated shrew."

"Don't be a dick," Carter bites back.

Right after Hawaii, a bunch of us were over at Carter and Suki's house. And Leo, after having *way* too many shots, walked into a bathroom without knocking and found Mara shaving her bikini line because we were all about to get in the new hot tub.

Screaming ensued. Profanities were exchanged. After she called him a desperate pervert, he may or may not have suggested she use a machete on her bush instead of a razor. And Mara has hated his guts ever since that night.

"Harry's making steak." Carter arches his brows. "You guys in or not?"

Leo runs a hand down his sweaty face, groaning. "Fine. But you better have some good bourbon if you expect me to put up with the Shrewnami."

"I can't make it, Lainey's getting here this evening and I'm making dinner at home."

"You could've brought her with you," Carter says. "Suki really wants to meet her."

"I'll bring her over soon. She's starting her research thing on Tuesday." I glance at my Apple Watch, tapping the screen to stop the time on my run. "I actually have to run so I can pick up some stuff and get showered before she gets here."

We run at a trail, and we start slowly making our way to the nearby parking lot.

A couple girls in little shorts and sports bras are approaching us on their run, both checking us out. The blond flicks her gaze to mine, biting her lower lip as she smiles. I nod and return my attention to my teammates.

"That's what I get for taking my shirt off, boys," I say under my breath.

Leo scoffs. "You're lucky I didn't take mine off; that's all I'm sayin'."

"What are you picking up?" Carter asks.

"What?"

"You said you have stuff to pick up before Lainey gets here. What is it?"

I lower my brows. "Don't know why it matters to you, but deodorant, Junior Mints and treats for Bruce."

"Junior Mints?"

I shrug. "For Lainey."

Knowing what's coming, Leo heads away from us with a wave. "See you tonight, man."

"See you," Carter says.

He turns to face me. "You're doing it."

I play dumb. "Doing what?"

"You know goddamn well what, Bash. What I told you at least ten fucking times not to do. You're trying to win her over so she'll leave her fiancé and then you'll decide you don't want her."

Aggravation flares in my chest. "Bullshit. I'd never do that to Lainey. We've been friends since we were kids. Eric's still one of my closest friends. He'd chop me into a thousand pieces if I hurt his sister."

He puts his palms up. "I don't know if you even realize you're doing it, but I know you well. You don't want her, but you don't want anyone else to have her, either."

I take off my baseball hat and rake a hand through my sweaty hair, then put it back on backward. "I don't want her, and I don't want *Shane* to have her. I care about her and I don't want to see her make the biggest mistake of her life."

"Uh-huh. So when what's her name texts and asks if she can come over so you can fuck her brains out, you'll say yes, even if Lainey is there?"

I hesitate. "Probably not, because that's pretty fucking rude when I have a guest."

"That's not why."

He's so full of shit and incapable of admitting when he's wrong. I take out my car keys, eager to get in my truck and drive away from this conversation.

"Get off my dick. I have to go." I flip him off and turn toward my truck. "Same time tomorrow?"

"Yep."

Carter gets in his dad-mobile—a Yukon. A star suncatcher his youngest niece Hallie made for him hangs from his rearview mirror, sparkling when it catches sunlight. I don't think he ever would have gotten married and had kids if his sister hadn't passed away. It's sadly ironic that the best thing that ever happened to him was because of the worst thing that ever happened to him.

I'm proud of him. Nothing means more to him than Suki and the girls. We're the kind of friends who say what's really on our minds, so I'm not pissed that he thinks I want Lainey to want me.

She used to want me, but that was a long time ago. Now we're both adults and she's important to me, but only in a friendly way. That's why I want her to dump Shitty Shane. He doesn't get her.

Someday, years from now, some other man will

see how bright, brilliant and funny she is. I'll shake his hand and wish him well.

Probably. Thinking about it is only making me do a Clint Eastwood scowl because she's still so young and I don't want her to settle down anytime soon.

That has to be it.

———

A FEW HOURS LATER, my dog Bruce goes to the window, barking at Lainey's old silver car. I've been watching for her from the front of my house, and when I walk out my front door, Bruce follows.

She's only been to my house a couple times when she's come with Eric to see my games, but I swear my dog recognizes her. She parks her car and gets out, giving Bruce her full attention.

He eats it up, his whole back end wagging. It's a problem that I'm kind of feeling the same way.

Her shoulder-length red hair is up in a little ponytail and she's wearing green-rimmed sunglasses.

She makes her simple gray V-neck T-shirt and cutoff jean shorts look good. Damn good.

The girl who always had at least one scraped-up

knee every summer, if not two, is now a woman. She has been for a while, but I guess I only noticed recently that she's not Little Lainey anymore.

I can't let on that I find her sexy as hell. Not only would Eric flip his shit, she would, too. She used to have a thing for me and I shot her down.

She moved on. And I'm fine with that—as long as she's not moving on with Shane.

CHAPTER TWO

Lainey

I'M BARELY OUT of my old Camry when Bash's dog, Bruce Wayne, comes out to greet me, drool flying from his mouth as he runs.

I bend, smiling at the huge gray Great Dane. "Hey, Brucey!"

He prances in a couple of excited circles, then shakes his butt as I rub his back and head. A gentle giant, he's a hundred and sixty pounds of well-trained cuddle bug.

"Hey, you made it."

My heart does a little leap when I see my brother's longtime best friend walking down the wide stone stairs of his home's front entrance. He's not my crush anymore, but my nervous system didn't get the memo. Bash is wearing gray shorts, a light-blue polo and—damn him—a backward baseball hat.

Adrenaline floods my bloodstream and my heart rate kicks up as he approaches, grinning lazily. I reason with myself. It's not really butterflies in my stomach—it's blood diverting from my digestive system toward my organs and muscles.

That backward baseball hat and grin still get me every time, even after all these years.

"Leave her alone, Bruce."

His distinctive gruff baritone voice stimulates the butterflies to flap even harder. He used to deejay at the high school radio station, and I never missed a second of his airtime. I had it so bad for him, even at age twelve.

He's six foot two and I'm five foot five, so when he hugs me, my face only reaches his shoulder. It's kind of like hugging a brick wall, his broad chest and shoulders hard with muscle. But brick walls don't smell like eucalyptus and rich, woody amber.

I pull back, overwhelmed by being so close to my

childhood crush, smelling his cologne and feeling his pecs.

"Did you know amber comes from fossilized tree resin?" I blurt, trying to get my racing heart to calm. "It takes thousands of years for the scent to develop. That's why perfume makers combine other scents to replicate amber."

A corner of Bash's mouth lifts in amusement. "No, I didn't know that."

I've always loved science, and Bash knows that. But I can't have him thinking I just randomly spit out science factoids.

"Your cologne has notes of amber in it," I explain. "That's what made me think of that."

"Amber, huh?"

I nod since talking isn't going so well for me right now. Guilt stabs me in the gut because I'm only supposed to get butterflies for Shane, my fiancé.

A glance around the driveway of Bash's house brings me back to reality. This is where I humiliated myself seven years ago. My adrenal medulla hits the brakes on the flow of epinephrine into my system. *Finally.*

"I better get my stuff inside."

"I'll bring your stuff in. Go grab a drink and sit down."

That—that *right there*—is what makes it so hard for me to kill those butterflies Bash gives me. He's a gentleman. Always holding doors and bringing me drinks. Even on that horrible day seven years ago, he did everything he could to try to make me feel better.

Not that any of it worked. I can still remember every giant landscaping boulder in his yard I wanted to crawl under that day and never return from.

"I've got it," I assure him. "Some of this stuff is staying in the car because it's going to the lab."

I blow a stray strand of hair out of my face.

"Why didn't Shane pack your car?"

A wall of defensiveness pops up inside me. Bash is always full of questions about Shane, and every one of them insinuates that he's lacking.

"He was busy."

"Busy with what?"

A video game tournament, but I'm not going to mention that. I just cut Bash a glare.

"I'm not a woman who needs a big, strong man taking care of me so I don't break a sweat."

A small snort escapes him. "Good thing, since Shane's about a buck sixty."

"Bash." I fold my arms and push out a hip. "Can

you not start your shit before I'm even inside the house?"

He puts his palms up. "Fine. Tell me what to carry in and I'll do it."

"Start with the mouthy hockey player. Set his ass down on the couch and leave him there for the rest of the day."

I open the passenger-side back seat door of my car and reach for the tall, rectangular black suitcase my dad loaned me. Bash's longer arm shoots past mine, his hand wrapping around the handle.

"I've got it, Lane. There's Malibu and pineapple juice in the kitchen. Go make yourself a drink."

I hesitate. Am I pissed that he's trying to coddle me or touched that he made sure to have the ingredients of my favorite drink on hand?

I don't even know. An argument with Shane before I left has me off balance. He was busy with friends last night, which was fine, but he wanted me to come by his place before I left, and he told me to plan on staying for at least half an hour.

It was because he wanted sex. I felt like an afterthought, so I told him I didn't have time. He didn't take it well.

"Thanks, but I don't drink in the afternoon," I tell Bash. "And I have to be sharp tomorrow."

He pulls out the suitcase that I struggled to lift into the car, easily holding it in one hand.

"What else?"

"My other stuff is in the trunk; let me open it."

I pop open my trunk and he surveys the boxes and three fully stuffed bags.

"The boxes stay in the car. The ones in the back seat stay, too. Everything else I'm bringing in."

I reach for a bag.

"Stop. I'm carrying your shit in."

The stern note in his voice stops me. I'm sweating on this ninety-degree afternoon because the air conditioning in my car is broken. This isn't a hill I need to die on.

"Okay, thanks."

I open the front door for him and walk into the kitchen with Bruce while he carries my things to an upstairs bedroom.

Even though I've been here a few times with Eric, I'm still awestruck by Bash's house. We grew up in a very middle-class neighborhood in Columbus. There were houses with weed-filled cracks in drive-ways and window air conditioning units humming along in the summer. Tractor tires doubled as planters.

Bash's house is the nicest I've ever been in.

Someone back home said he paid two million dollars for it. It's huge, with dark hardwood floors and tons of windows. The biggest room on the main level, which I'd call a living room, is an open two stories, with automatic blinds on the floor-to-ceiling windows, lots of comfortable leather furniture and framed black-and-white photos on the walls.

The room is open to the kitchen, which is bright and modern. It has white cabinets and white marble counters, six stools lined up at a massive island. The stainless appliances look like they belong in the kitchen of a gourmet restaurant.

The counters are mostly empty. There's a glass jar beside the stove filled with treats for Bruce, and a crock with utensils on the other side of the stove, and that's about it.

I can't wait to try out his Wolf oven. The only thing I cook or bake is sourdough bread, and I'm slightly obsessed with it. I take my starter out of the oversized bag that comes everywhere with me and set it on the back of an empty span of kitchen counter.

"What's that?"

I turn as Bash walks into the room. "That's Dough Goldberg."

He arches a brow.

"My sourdough starter. I'm going to make so many things in that oven. Bread, pizza crust, muffins —I even have a recipe for granola."

Leaning back on the island, Bash crosses his arms. "You're going to love Harry."

"Who's that?"

"One of Suki's best friends. She's my teammate Carter's wife. I spend a lot of time at their house. My trainer has me on a high-protein, low-carb diet. I have a chef who comes here to make me stuff."

I lower my brows. "So you won't eat my sourdough?"

"I'll have some. But I have to watch my sugar."

"I'll make you some bread. And granola. Sourdough is really good for your gut health. You need microbe diversity and you can't get that from just protein and vegetables. Tell your trainer I said that."

He grins. "You're selling it so well. Now I'm craving a microbe sandwich."

I know he's joking, but I take science very seriously. "Did you know that ninety percent of serotonin is made in your gut? You know what serotonin is, right?"

"Yes, Lainey. I know what serotonin is."

"And serotonin levels can contribute to depression and anxiety. Bread can literally make people happier."

He walks over to the fridge. "I believe it. I'm a grouchy fucker when I'm not getting any."

He means carbs, Lainey. Not getting any carbs. Stop thinking about Bash naked. Seriously—stop.

I clear my throat, willing away the warmth on my cheeks. "Thanks for letting me stay here. It's saving me a ton of money. I want to pay you something, though."

"Absolutely not."

"But--"

"No." He takes a long pull from the stainless water bottle he just took out of the fridge. "Make yourself at home because this is your home as long as you want to be here. Just credit me with your success in your Nobel acceptance speech."

I laugh at the thought. Bash's smile fades away.

"Seriously, though. I think what you do is badass. Using your work to help people."

"That's the goal."

"I'm proud of you."

The warmth in my cheeks intensifies. Damn my fair skin. It's like a neon billboard of my emotions. And the admiration in Bash's tone and gaze is making me warm all over.

It's what I dreamed of every day for years. I wanted to be special to him. He admires my work, though. Not me, Lainey, the woman.

And that's okay. I moved on a long time ago. Bash is my friend now, and he's a dear one. I have Shane.

"Thanks," I manage.

"You want a drink?"

"No, I had a Dr Pepper on the way here."

He groans. "You're still drinking that shit?"

"Daily. Dr Pepper is my general practitioner. He's an absolute boss, but the pelvic exams get a little invasive."

With a grin, he says, "Come on, I'll show you your room."

He leads the way up the open, curved stairway with an intricately carved walnut railing. The walls upstairs are bare, but the space is still light and airy.

I've only been up here when I was staying the night with Eric after watching one of Bash's games. We did that twice during his first season playing for Cleveland. After that, I started dating Shane, and he didn't want me coming to Bash's games.

"You're in here."

He walks into the first door on the right. I stayed in this room the other times we came here. It has the same dark wood floors as the main level, with three windows and a king-size bed that belongs in a luxury hotel. There are burgundy pillows lined up neatly and the white comforter is perfectly smooth, without a single wrinkle.

My bags are already inside the walk-in closet.

This room has its own bathroom, and I peek into the doorway, making sure the gorgeous bathtub is still there.

"I've always wanted to take a bath in that tub."

I never had time for it the two times I stayed here. We got to Bash's house really late after his games, usually after midnight, and we were up early the next morning for breakfast.

"Go for it. I'm making roasted chicken and veggies for dinner tonight. Figured we'd stay in."

Here comes the dopamine rush. I'm over my crush on Bash—really—but him cooking dinner and talking about us having a night in is doing things to me.

Unexpected things.

"That sounds great," I say. "I need to call Shane and I think I'll unpack."

"I'll leave you to it."

He leaves the room, pulling the door closed softly behind him.

I sit down on the edge of the bed and look at my ring. My engagement ring. I'm marrying Shane in five months, and I'm happy about it.

I am. Standing up, I go over to the closet to unpack, typing out a quick text to let my fiancé know I made it. I told Bash I was going to call him just so I could escape from the unexpected rush I was getting over him.

Shane wouldn't pick up right now because of his video game tournament. And I'm still mad at him, anyway. I definitely won't be telling Bash that, though. He doesn't need any more reasons to dislike Shane.

CHAPTER THREE

Bash

THE NEXT MORNING, my hand freezes in midair when Lainey walks into the kitchen, my mug of green tea in limbo.

"Good morning," she says breezily.

"Morning."

She's wearing fitted black pants and a sleeveless, vibrant green shirt with a scoop neckline, the outfit hugging her curves. Her thick hair is sleek and straight, the ends just brushing over her shoulders. She has makeup on today, her eyes rimmed in dark shades and the light pink of her lips matching her cheeks.

The only time I've seen her like this was at her engagement party to Shitty Shane in June. She had on a blue dress that night and her hair was swept into a neat knot at the nape of her neck. Shitty Shane wore jeans and an ugly polo. Who's surprised?

It's a shock to my system to see Lainey looking sexy, and it's even more of one to see her looking that way *in my kitchen*. When she came to my games a couple of years ago, she was wearing a Crush hoodie and jeans.

"There's apple kale and carrot ginger juice," I say as she opens the fridge.

She looks over her shoulder at me and smiles. "I'm not taking your juice. I'm just grabbing my water bottle."

"No, take it. Seriously. I had the chef make extra since I knew you were coming."

She furrows her brow. "I don't want to spoil my midmorning breakfast of frosted cherry Pop-Tarts."

"Jesus. With a Dr Pepper, I'm sure. Don't you study this stuff and know better? How are Pop-Tarts for gut health?"

"Not great, Mom. Sugar thins the mucus lining of the gut and it can actually make my IBS worse. I have no idea when I'll be home, but I'll grab dinner on my way."

I cup my hands around my mouth as she heads for the door. "Eat some protein today."

She looks back at me. "Is there protein in Twix bars?"

I set my mug on the counter and glare at her. "Are you fucking kidding me?"

She grins. "Yeah. I'll have a salad for lunch. Promise. With protein."

After slinging her enormous bag over her shoulder, she blows me a kiss and leaves through the door that connects the kitchen to the garage.

I sigh heavily, then take a sip of my tea. That was really fucking...domesticated. Add a kiss and an ass slap at the end and we could've been a couple. I don't know what to do with that, because I'm not a domesticated guy.

My home isn't open to women I sleep with. And I don't expect to go to their homes, either, but I have before if that's what worked best. If I want to spend the night with a woman and I know about it ahead of time, I book a nice hotel room.

Lainey isn't one of those women, though. She's...Lainey. Eric's sister. She's like family.

I shake it off, walking over to the fridge to get out some eggs and juice. Carter, Leo and I have leg day with our trainer, Ollie, today. I need to get fueled up and mentally set for it.

———

LEO SPRINTS ABOUT FOUR YARDS, then jerks to a halt, dropping to his hands and lying face down in the grass, then bounces back up and jumps high in the air.

I follow, not wasting any energy on bitching, though I want to. Leo's a grinder, and he's a beast of one. He's not a polished player who just fires goal after goal into the net, like Carter. He's the work-horse of the first offensive line, and he's in the best shape of anyone on our team. Leo uses his imposing size, strength and speed to disrupt our opponents.

He checks. He forechecks. He boards. Leo is the most relentless grinder I've ever played with, and he's arguably the most important member of the line he, Carter and I make up.

His aggression is what keeps Leo's spot on our team secure, and he stays sharp. He may not score a ton of goals, but he makes opportunities for me and Carter to.

His physicality makes him the worst person to be behind in mirror drills. We're on the football-field-sized grass area outside our team's training facility, and I drew the short straw in this round of drills.

Carter is mirroring Ollie on the other side of the field. Ollie focuses entirely on speed. He stops, starts, and dodges to the side, Carter repeating every movement from about ten feet behind him.

Leo, though, won't just do a typical hockey mirror drill. He adds karate kicks, push-ups, hurdles, burpees and even the occasional backflip.

By the time he turns around and backflips across the finish line, I'm practically wheezing. I shake my head, unwilling to risk hurting myself with a backflip when I'm this gassed.

"Did you keep up?" Leo asks me, grinning.

I flip him off.

"We'll switch leaders after you guys get a drink," Ollie says.

My breathing has returned to normal by the time I get over to the bench where our water bottles are. I swipe mine and take a long swig from it.

"How was the cookout last night?" I ask.

"Yeah, how was it, Leo?" Carter scowls at him.

Leo shrugs. "Fine. The steaks were killer."

Carter rolls his eyes. "I thought Mara might actually punch you."

He shrugs. "She's a loose cannon."

"Because you intentionally bait her."

"She makes it too easy."

Carter shakes his head and turns to me. "How was dinner with Lainey?"

"Good."

Leo screws the cap back on his water bottle and stretches into a lunge. "How many times did you criticize her fiancé?"

"Only twice. I was feeling reserved."

"How was it seeing her?" Carter asks.

I feign nonchalance. "Same as always. Lainey's Lainey."

"Just a pal you hang out with, right?" Leo says dryly. "Just like us."

"Well, she's not a dick, so...not just like you guys."

"Let's go!" Ollie calls from across the field.

Carter and I set down our water bottles.

"Bring her over tomorrow night," he says. "Suki won't let up about meeting her."

"If neither of us has plans, I will."

He hums a single note of laughter. "You already know you don't have plans and she just got to town yesterday, so she doesn't, either. You just don't want Suki, Mara, Dex, and Harry to see you with her because you know they'll see right through you."

Agitation tightens against my breastbone.

"Suck my dick. You don't know what you're talking about. She tried to get with me once and I told her no. If you guys say anything that embarrasses her, I'll be fucking pissed. I mean it."

"No one will do that. You know Suki and her friends."

We walk over to Ollie, who's warming up with jump squats.

"I'll bring her over, but you need to tell Suki that if anyone pries for information, we're leaving and I won't bring her back."

Carter frowns at me. "Yeah, because you're better at making people feel welcome than my wife is? Cut the shit."

If he thinks anyone is being critical of Suki, Carter turns into a defensive caveman. I drop the subject and go to the spray-painted white line in the grass, where we start mirror drills.

Leo yawns dramatically behind me. "Do you need me awake for this, Bash? Or can I take a nap during?"

I take off my baseball hat and run a hand through my sweaty hair, replace the hat and give him a shit-eating grin. "You're fucked, man. I stashed some sticks and pucks and nets down there. I'm gonna shoot goals and we all know you can't mirror that shit."

He narrows his eyes. "So you want to stand still, granddad? Are we going to practice sitting on the bench, too?"

"Let's go!" Ollie calls, already following behind Carter.

I spin around and give Leo double middle fingers, then start sprinting. This drill is good for me. It takes all my energy to do it, so there's no room left to think about the way Lainey's round ass looked in those pants this morning.

Not much room, anyway. It creeps into my mind every few minutes, and so does a replay of her blowing me a kiss.

So weird. I have no idea where these thoughts are coming from because, like I told Carter and Leo, Lainey's *Lainey*. My childhood best friend's younger sister. She's pretty much the last person whose ass I should be thinking about.

CHAPTER FOUR

Lainey

MY JAW HITS the floor when I see an enormous pink
pig waddling over to us, his curly tail...wagging?

"Darling!" Bash bends to pet the pig, who, to be
fair, he warned me about.

But I had no idea his teammate's pet would be the
cutest thing I've ever seen. The logo on the back of
the Cleveland Crush T-shirt he's wearing is
stretched from him filling every free inch of the
shirt. He's snuffling at Bash, blissed out with his
head in the air as Bash rubs his back thoroughly.

"Is he smiling?" I murmur.

Darling turns his snuffling my way, the little

snorting noises melting me. I lean down and let him snuffle at my face.

"Don't worry, he's not the ugliest dude she's kissed recently," Bash says to someone.

I stand and flick a glare at him.

A tall man with brown hair and a handsome face ignores Bash's jab, putting a hand on my shoulder. "Lainey, I'm Carter. It's great to finally meet you. Sorry about our pushy swine."

"Are you kidding? I love him."

A beautiful woman with her light-brown hair in a messy bun approaches us, her smile radiant.

"Lainey, at last we meet." She hugs me and I catch a hint of her light floral perfume. "I'm Suki Stanton, Carter's wife."

"It's so nice to meet you."

I feel at ease already. After hugging me, Suki puts an arm around my shoulder and leads me into the main living area of their home.

It's beautiful. The gray and navy leather furniture is modern but still looks comfortable. Framed artwork that looks like it was made by children decorates the walls, one of the pictures of Darling, the pig. There are a few big tropical plants in corners and a shelf with pothos trailing down both sides, the potted plants on the shelf in colorful pots.

Laughter sounds from another room.

"Don't doubt me, foolish mortal!"

The playful comment—made by a man—makes me smile. Suki rolls her eyes, but she's smiling, too.

"My friends are kind of a lot."

My smile widens. "Perfect. I'm kind of a lot, too."

She turns to Bash. "I like her."

"What's not to like?"

Suki folds her hands and puts them beneath her chin, giving me a hopeful look. "Do you, by any chance, like trivia?"

"Are you kidding? I was on the scholastic bowl team for six years and I'm a total science nerd. I *love* trivia."

She hops up and down in a little dance. "I knew it as soon as I saw you! Come meet the other Smartinis."

Bash lowers his brows, confused. "The who?"

"You already know all of them; it's my trivia team."

"Ah."

Suki leads me into their home's formal dining room, which has modern navy and white decor, the rectangular farmhouse-style table seating twelve. Two men, a woman and two girls are sitting at the table, and they all look over as we walk into the room.

"Guys, this is Lainey. Lainey, this is Harry, Mara, Dex, Charlotte and Hallie."

Harry, Mara and Dex all get up to hug me and greet me warmly. Then, the younger girl pushes a curl out of her face and comes over to hug me, too.

"I just love Darling," I say.

"Me too. He's my best friend."

I melt. "And you're...Charlotte or Hallie?"

"Hallie. You can be on my team if you want."

"I'd love to."

I lock eyes with Bash, who's standing on the other side of the table, and he winks at me. The butterflies flutter in response, but I tamp them down.

It's just a habit for me to swoon over his very existence. He was my crush for years. I have an entire notebook I was using as a diary as a teenager that's filled with dreamy Sebastian Stone musings.

I wrote *Mrs. Sebastian Stone* in that notebook hundreds of times, and I wrote out fantasy dates for us. He was drafted into pro hockey right out of high school, so from the time I was fourteen, I imagined him calling me onto center ice in front of a crowded arena of screaming fans and announcing to the world that he loved me. Then he'd get down on one knee and propose.

After The Incident, though, I wised up. I started dreaming of becoming an independent, accomplished scientist who signed her name, *Dr. Delaney Morris*, instead of *Mrs. Sebastian Stone*.

"How many hearts does an octopus have?" Dex asks the girls.

"We're doing practice trivia," Mara explains to me.

Suki takes Bash's shoulders and guides him over to the side of the table I'm on.

"Harry and I need to finish up dinner. You take over for me, Bash, and Carter can take over for Harry."

"Do you want help?" I offer.

She waves a hand. "Nah, there's not much left to do."

"What do you think, girls?" Bash asks Hallie and Charlotte. "How many hearts in an octopus?"

"One?" Charlotte guesses with a shrug.

"I think eight," Hallie says. "One in each leg."

"We've got a real scientist on our team. See what she thinks."

Charlotte's eyes widen with admiration. "You're a scientist?"

"I'm a microbiologist."

"Whoa."

"I love that," Dex says. "Tell us about your work."

He's very good-looking, fit and clean-shaven, wearing a T-shirt that says, "I'm not gay, but my boyfriend is." I like him immediately.

"Well, today, I started working on a project with a professor at Cleveland State. We're studying the microbiome." I break it down further so the girls will understand. "The food we eat travels through the digestive system, and one of the places it goes is our large intestines. There are trillions of microorganisms there—fungi, bacteria and viruses—and they make up our microbiome. Ninety percent of the serotonin in our bodies, which is the feel-good chemical that makes us all happy, is made in that microbiome. I'm isolating and studying a strain of bacteria that may help treat anxiety."

"Seriously?" Dex puts his elbow on the table and rests his chin on his fist. "That sounds fascinating."

"I think it is."

"Will you be a Smartini?" Mara asks me. "Please?"

Suki answers from the kitchen. "I already asked her; she's in! I'll get you a T-shirt, Lainey."

I can't believe how quickly they welcomed me

into their group. Though I'm not sure what it means just yet.

"What do I need to do to be a Smartini?"

Mara grins at me. "You have to be fucking fabulous and smart—which, done. And you have to come to trivia with us on Tuesday nights at the Tap House."

Dex looks at Mara, his brows pushed together with concern. "She also has to be ruthless. We show no mercy to other teams."

"Right." Mara turns to me. "You can be ruthless, right?"

"Ruthless is my middle name."

Hallie laughs. "That's a weird middle name."

I feel Bash's gaze on me, and I glance at him. Warmth and pride swim in his eyes. The flutter in my stomach returns because I'm not used to Bash looking at me this way.

"Lainey, do you know how many hearts an octopus has?" Charlotte asks me.

Grateful for the distraction, I say, "Three."

"Is the plural of octopus octopi?" Carter asks me.

"It's octopuses."

"Lainey, geez." Bash puts his hands over Hallie's ears. "There are children present."

Carter laughs. "They hear a lot worse than octopuses from me. And Aunt Mara."

Mara nods. "Aunt Mara needs her mouth washed out with soap. Preferably by Jason Momoa."

"Okay, people!" Suki calls from the kitchen. "Dinner's ready!"

Everyone makes their way into the kitchen, where Harry and Suki have prepared an elaborate taco bar on the island. There are hard shells, soft shells, tortilla chips, grilled steak, chicken and shrimp, lettuce, tomatoes, onions and several kinds of cheese and sauce.

And best of all, a heaping bowl of fresh guacamole. There are also bowls of rice and beans for the side and a big glass pitcher of margaritas.

"Lainey?" Suki offers as she pours a margarita. "Can I get you one?"

"Not tonight, but thanks. I have an early morning."

"I want to hear more about your work sometime. I had no idea the bacteria in our intestines could have anything to do with mental health."

This is my catnip—people who like hearing about what I do. I'm passionate about it.

"Anytime."

A teenage girl comes into the room, AirPods in her ears. She silently makes herself a plate.

"That's our oldest, Olivia," Suki says. "I'd introduce you, but she's a teenager, so she can't even."

I laugh. "I get it. I'll meet her another time."

Carter walks over to Suki and puts a palm on her lower back, his other hand on her hip as he pulls her closer and kisses her. "This looks amazing, babe."

She smiles up at him, radiating happiness. "I didn't try to cook the steak. I left that to Harry."

"You ruined it *one time*," Harry says. "You need to get back on that horse."

"She has something better than a horse to ride now," Mara quips.

"What?" Hallie gives Suki a questioning look. "What do you have that's better than a horse?"

"Aunt Mara can explain," Suki says breezily.

Hallie turns to Mara, who smiles brightly. "I meant the wave of life, honey. She's riding the wave of life. It's metaphorical."

I make myself two tacos with grilled chicken and veggies, avoiding the cheese and steak because I don't think they'll agree with my stomach.

When I'm back in the dining room, Bash comes in carrying a plate loaded up with steak, chicken and veggies.

"This is okay for you, right?" he murmurs.

"Yeah, it's fine." My cheeks warm. "It looks like you're eating for three."

He grins. "I'm a growing boy."

I appreciate his concern about my health, but at the same time, it's humiliating. I've had irritable bowel syndrome since I was fourteen. I have to be careful about what I eat and always know where the nearest bathroom is.

Who could blame Bash for not being interested in me? No man's checklist for his dream woman includes *prone to sudden diarrhea*. It's why Shane and I have never spent a night together. I have my place and he has his, and I'm nervous about us living together once we're married.

Carter sits down across from us at the dining table, his plate as loaded up as Bash's.

"So Lainey, anytime you're ready to share embarrassing childhood stories about Bash, I'm all ears."

I glance at Bash and laugh. "I always thought Bash and Eric were the coolest. I don't really know anything embarrassing about him."

He knows lots of embarrassing things about me, but I know I can trust him not to blab. They're ancient history now.

"Oh, but there was the mustache." I glance at Bash, who rolls his eyes. "That was pretty hilarious."

Carter's face lights with amusement. "Tell me more about this mustache."

"What year was that?" I ask Bash? "Were you a sophomore?"

He nods. "It was for my team's no-shave November. But since I have more male hormones flowing through this honed body of mine, my stache was more impressive than anyone else's."

I wrinkle my nose. "Was it, though?"

"It got me a date with a college girl. She thought I was twenty."

My eleven-year-old self would have been crushed to know he went out with a college girl. Or any girl, honestly. I cried over the homecoming and prom photos my mom took of Eric and Bash with their dates because I wanted to be the one next to Bash more than anything.

"Then she saw that you looked like one of those hairless cats between your legs?" Mara quips.

"Nah, I didn't make it past the first date without a driver's license."

After dinner and dessert, which is a decadent flourless cake I don't dare risk eating, we return to trivia. Carter and Bash go into Carter's study for a while, but I still feel very comfortable with Suki and her friends. By the time I leave, I have all their numbers in my phone, and they have mine, too.

"Did you have fun?" Bash asks on the drive home.

"I had an amazing time. Thanks for bringing me."

"You'll be seeing a lot of them while you're here. That's pretty much my Cleveland family if you add in a few more of my teammates."

I remember a text from Shane earlier. "Hey, Shane wants to come visit this weekend. Is it okay if he stays at your place?"

He presses his lips together, his jaw tensing. After a few seconds, he says, "Yeah."

I knew he didn't like Shane, but I wasn't expecting this. "We can get a hotel room."

"No, it's fine."

"Are you ever going to give him a chance?"

He shrugs. "He's not good enough for you, Lane. That's never going to change."

I exhale heavily and turn to look out the window because there's no point in continuing this conversation. It ends the same way every time.

My own brother is okay with me marrying Shane. I can't for the life of me figure out why his best friend has a problem with it.

CHAPTER FIVE

Bash

"You've got a great setup here for a pool and hot tub combo. Here's my card if you ever want to talk about options. I own a pool construction business."

Shitty Shane Thompson passes Coach Turner a business card, a flicker of embarrassment passing over Lainey's face. I'm giving Shane the Clint Eastwood *get off my lawn* squint, even though the fucker deserves a dick punch.

"Let's not talk shop today," Lainey says lightly. "Where should I put the dip I brought?"

Lainey, Shane and I just got to my head coach's house for a team cookout, which happened to be scheduled for the day Shane was coming to visit. My choices were to invite Shane and Lainey to come with me or leave them at my house alone, where he would've tried to have sex with her.

That's not really a choice at all.

"I'll take that," Coach's wife Angie says. "Oh, it looks delicious!"

Our head coach, Noel Turner, is the polar opposite of his wife. She's a bubbly tan blonde and he's a grouchy dick who's graying at his temples. Said with love, of course. I wouldn't want to play hockey for anyone but him, but his coaching style isn't for everyone.

He pulls no punches and expects hard work, but he works just as hard as his players. He's not a warm, encouraging sort. When he praises his players, we know we earned it and he means it.

"You keeping the pounds off, Stone?" he asks me wryly, clapping me on the shoulder.

"He's Fatman," our goalie Isaac says from nearby, not missing a beat.

I roll my eyes. "Shit, man, your voice is about ten octaves too high to even try saying that."

Leo walks up and puts an arm around me, doing his imitation of the kid from Shrek. "Do the roar."

It's not a roar, but that's what he says when he wants me to do the Batman thing.

"I don't like being objectified," I gripe. "I'm more than a sexy voice, a killer body and a perfect face."

That draws laughs and even a rare quirk of the lips from Coach. I glance at Lainey, who's giving me a warm smile.

"Do it, Stone," Isaac calls out.

"I'll do it once. After that, you'll need to discuss terms with my agent." I clear my throat, drawing it out because I like having Lainey's undivided attention.

"I'm Batman," I say gruffly.

"Outstanding." Leo claps my shoulder. "Never gets old."

"It does after a decade or so," Shane quips.

Leo and Isaac look at him, both unamused. Shane puts up his palms.

"Hey, don't knock my teeth out. I went to high school with him. It was a joke."

"You guys went to school together?" Coach asks.

I nod. "I've known Shane since he wasn't balding. That was a long, long time ago."

My coach and teammates in earshot freeze, like they don't know if it's okay to laugh. Shane puts an arm around Lainey's shoulders.

"Yeah, I still remember when you got cut from the high school hockey team junior year," he says.

I shrug, my fingers twitching at the thought of landing just one solid punch on his smarmy face. If someone would take a photo of his expression as I'm about to hit him, piss running down his leg as he panics, I'd make it my phone wallpaper.

"Turned out okay for me."

"Drinks," Lainey says brightly. "Why don't we get some drinks?"

She takes Shane's hand and leads him over to the outdoor bar, which is being worked by two bartenders today.

Coach Turner was a legendary player before becoming a coach, and his home is spectacular. There are floor-to-ceiling glass doors on the massive sunroom that slide open, making the space indoor and outdoor in the summer. Several patios have seating areas, one of them with a long dining table that seats twenty people.

The landscaping is all professionally maintained, with fountains gurgling around the perimeter of the yard. There's a guest cottage that puts the little two-room cottage in my yard to shame. It has a bedroom, a poolroom, another bar, a full kitchen, a library and a big living room.

I'd love to have a place like this someday, with kids in the yard to play catch with. It wasn't something I thought about much until I saw Carter pretty much become a dad to three girls overnight.

The transition hasn't been perfect. But now that I know each of his girls and I've heard him talk about their vulnerabilities and quirks, I can't imagine him without them. Suki and the girls are his team now. He'd walk through fire for any of them, and even though there are hard days, I sometimes envy the adoring looks and stolen kisses I see between him and his wife. Hallie thinks Carter hung the moon. Olivia and Charlotte ask him for advice and beg him to take them out for one-on-one coffee dates.

I assumed marriage and kids were way down the road for me, but maybe not.

"Hey."

I look over my shoulder and find Carter giving me a half glare.

"You should make sure the people you invited here don't feel like outsiders," he scolds.

I scoff, speaking under my breath. "Shane can kiss my entire asshole. Can't you see what a douchebag he is?"

He follows my gaze over to Lainey, who's looking

at Shane as he talks animatedly to Suki, probably about pool maintenance, his favorite topic.

"Have you let her know how you feel about her?" he asks in a low tone.

I pinch my brows together. "It's how I feel about *him* that's an issue."

He rolls his eyes, exasperated. "I'm a grown-ass adult who has plenty of childish bullshit to deal with from my own kids. I'm done dancing around this. It's your feelings for her that are creating your feelings for him. You get that, right?"

I grunt my disagreement. "I just don't want her to make a huge mistake with him. She can do better."

He holds up a palm. "Your jealousy is so fucking transparent, man. I saw the way you looked at her at my house the other day."

Tension knots in my stomach. I don't like this conversation. It's one thing having an attraction to Lainey buried deep inside, where I don't have to actually acknowledge it. Being called out on it is different.

I look over both shoulders, not finding anyone in earshot. But still, I nod to an empty part of the yard and Carter follows me there.

Making sure we're standing somewhere no one can read my lips, I take a deep breath. This is harder than I thought it would be. I practically whisper even though we're a hundred feet from anyone else.

"Lainey had a crush on me when we were growing up. But she was Eric's little sister. She's four years younger than us. And she made a play for me once. I broke her heart and she finally moved on. So yeah, there's been an attraction to her for a while now, but I can't..." I look away. "It wouldn't be fair for me to tell her. I just don't want her to marry Shane. He's not good enough for her."

"Okay, but what if...you had a mature conversation with her instead of making fun of his receding hairline in front of your teammates? Just throwing that out there as an option."

I cross my arms and huff out a heavy sigh. "I've tried. She gets defensive and says I don't know him."

"You need to be honest with her about your feelings."

I shake my head adamantly against that. "No way. She'd either smack me or start crying. Maybe both."

My team captain squints at me with a look that says, *Are you fucking serious right now?* "I think you can handle it, Bash."

"Right. Because you love it when Suki gets all emotional."

He scrubs a hand down his face and looks up at the sky. "I don't love it, but I deal with it."

"Daddy!"

Carter looks over at Hallie, who's smiling and holding a hockey stick.

"Come play hockey with us!"

"She just called you Daddy."

"Yeah, she started that recently. I don't know if she realizes it yet, but if she said, 'Daddy, will you buy me a Porsche?' there'd be one in the driveway by the end of the day."

My stoic, grouchy teammate is already walking toward Hallie, the kids in the driveway cheering.

"We'll finish talking another time," Carter calls over his shoulder. "Go do what I told you to."

Fuck. I'd much rather play field hockey with the kids. Actually, I'd prefer lying down and letting the kids beat me with hockey sticks to being nice to Shane.

But for Lainey, I'll try.

I walk over to Lainey, Shane and Suki, my forced friendly look feeling super weird. It has to look weird. Shane makes me scowl—I can't help it.

Lainey gives me a quick, frosty glare that hits me right in the chest.

Fuck. I have to be nice to Shane and I'm stone-cold sober. I wait for a break in the conversation and say, "So, Shane, how's business? It's your busy season, isn't it?"

"Yeah, we can hardly keep up. I've been working every day, but I shifted some things around so I could come see my wifey-to-be."

It's hard to look like you're smiling casually while grinding your teeth until pain shoots through your jaw. If I had a can of beer in my hand right now, I'd crush it. Full or not. I can't stand the sound of him calling Lainey his wifey-to-be.

"Oh, that's right!" Suki smiles brightly. "You're engaged. Let's see that ring."

"You'll need a microscope to make out the diamond," I quip. "If you see a speck of dust on it, don't brush it away because that—"

Lainey silences me with a murderous look. "Bash, you have five seconds to get out of my sight before I clock you. I mean that with every fiber of my being."

I turn and go, heading for the closest bar. While I don't like Lainey being pissed at me, I'm not sorry. Eric told me he was floored when he saw Lainey's engagement ring, a simple silver band with a fleck of a diamond set into it.

She said it's perfect for her because when she works in a lab, a bigger diamond would only get in the way. Bullshit. She's just an apologist for her cheap-ass boyfriend.

I slide onto a stool at the bar next to Isaac, our starting goalie.

"How's it going?" he asks.

I grunt at him as the bartender approaches.

"I'll take a double shot of whiskey," I say.

"And there's my answer," Isaac says.

"I don't feel like talking."

"Fair enough." He holds his glass up and I clink mine against his.

"Cheers," he says.

"Yeah, whatever."

———

BY EVENING, I'm a little drunk. I drove us to the cookout in my Jeep Wrangler, and Lainey drives it back to my place. I play loud music so I don't have to listen to Shane. Lainey's definitely still angry, and even though I'm a happy drunk, I have to fight my urge to turn off the music and start an argument with her over Shane.

I need to wait until I'm sober.

The top down in my jeep, Lainey's red hair flies all over in the wind. When we're stopped at a light, she pulls it back into a ponytail, refusing to look at me.

By the time she pulls into my garage, I'm sure she's going to take me out back and beat me or something. There's fire in her eyes and her lips are pressed into a thin line.

She storms into the house, Shane smirking. I want to run him over so fucking bad. Just one time, with my truck.

When I follow Shane into the house, Lainey's petting Bruce, his tail wagging as he burrows the side of his face against her.

"Go to bed, Bash," Lainey says. "I'll feed Bruce and take him out."

I get a bottle of water from the fridge and take a big swig from it. "I'm fine. I'll take care of him."

"You're not fine."

I lock my gaze onto hers. "I know whether or not I'm fine, Lane."

"Uh..." Shane clears his throat. "I'm gonna go get my bags."

"You're in the last room on the left upstairs," I say.

Lainey's jaw comes unhinged. "No, he's in *my* room."

I shake my head, adamant. "It's my house and I

assign rooms. Lainey, you're in my room tonight and I'm on the couch."

"Oh, hell no," Lainey mutters.

No way am I listening to Shitty Shane bang my best friend's sister all weekend in my own goddamn house. I thought about it as soon as I agreed he could stay here, and this is the solution. Lainey will be in my bedroom on the main level, and from the couch, I'll be able to see if she leaves the room.

"Shane, go get your bags," Lainey says.

"Maybe we should just go to a hotel."

I scowl at him. "I said you can stay here. It just won't be a fuck fest. You aren't even married yet. Have some class, man."

Lainey sounds like a boiling teapot—and she looks like one, too.

"What is wrong with you, Bash?" She launches the words at me. "Why are you being such an asshole?"

"I'm just looking out for you."

I walk past her to the living room, where I lie down on the couch. Bruce follows, curling up at my feet. She's on his heels.

"I'm almost twenty-five, you know. I'm an adult and I'm engaged."

"Good for you. I'm almost twenty-nine. I'm an adult and I'm single."

I know I'm being obnoxious, but fuck it. Lainey is smart, beautiful and funny. She deserves to be treated like a fucking queen. And if she won't see reason, I'll sabotage her shitty relationship however I can.

"You're just being a mean asshole." She folds her arms and narrows her eyes at me.

I scramble into a sitting position, Bruce jumping into my lap. "He still had an active Tinder profile three months after you guys started dating, Lane. Good guys don't do that shit."

Her face reddens. "Eric told you that?"

"What the fuck, Lainey?" Shane demands, coming into the room. "You told your brother about that?"

Her eyes widen with alarm as I shoot up off the couch. I advance on Shane, pointing at him.

"Raise your voice to her again and see what happens, you son of a bitch. You don't get to be pissed at her about that! You should be groveling at her fucking feet!"

He looks past me to Lainey, his voice lower this time. "What else have you told them?"

My laugh is humorless. "What else is there to know, motherfucker?"

He shakes his head. "You know what, I'm just gonna go."

"Shane, don't," Lainey says.

"You know where the door is," I say sharply.

He turns to go and Lainey follows, giving me a withering look. It takes all my self-control not to follow them. Instead, I go to the front window, watching Shane's SUV as she follows him to it. If he even looks like he might lay a hand on her, I'll be on him so damn fast he won't know what hit him.

He gets inside and drives away without another word to her. Asshole.

Lainey comes back inside, tears on her face as she walks past me to go upstairs.

"Lane," I say softly. "Hey."

She won't even acknowledge me. I hear her bedroom door open and close upstairs, and I sit back down on the couch. Bruce lets out a quick, soft whine.

"Don't you start with me, too," I grumble.

He yowls, talking back. I ignore him, curling up on my side since I can't fit my entire body on the couch.

I'm feeling sober as fuck now. Even my dog is mad at me.

CHAPTER SIX

Lainey

"Hey." Sitting at the kitchen table, Bash looks up from his phone. "Good morning."

I flip him off. All I need is my water bottle and I'm leaving. I swipe it from the fridge, keeping my expression frosty.

We haven't spoken since Shane left Saturday. Shane is pretty much over it, but I'm not. I spent all day yesterday exploring Cleveland on my own. I checked out bookstores, coffee shops and boutiques. When I got back to Bash's with the carryout I'd picked up for dinner, I took it to my room.

I'm so ready to get back into the lab today. My shitty weekend was entirely Bash's fault, and if anything, I'm even more pissed off at him now than I was then.

"Come on, Lane. Do you want me to say I'm sorry?"

My plan to give him the silent treatment goes to shit, thanks to my temper.

"Why would I want that? You're not sorry! You'd just be saying it to placate me."

"Isn't the point that I'm willing to say it?"

Anger seeps out of my pores. It's not just anger at him but at myself, too. Because despite him being the worst person in the world, I can't help noticing the way his arms look in his T-shirt. His shoulders and biceps fill it. And he's wearing a backward baseball hat, which is my weakness.

On him only, which is even worse. Shane doesn't wear baseball hats, and when I asked him to wear one backward once, it did nothing for me.

But my own biochemistry hijacks me when I'm around Sebastian Stone. No matter how many times I tell myself I've moved on and I'm not attracted to him anymore, when I'm around him, my brain floods with phenylethylamine.

I can describe it scientifically, but the reality is like jumping off a cliff with my eyes closed. Racing heartbeat and dry mouth. Pounding pulse and inability to concentrate. It's terrifying but also exhilarating.

Why did I think living with him for an entire summer was a good idea? It's saving me money, but it's costing me peace. His few days' worth of unshaven, dark stubble is doing things to me. Making me sweat. Making my breasts feel heavier.

He stands up and walks over to me, the cedar and amber scents in his soap making my heart pound.

"I'll never think he's good enough for you," he says softly.

I shake my head. "He's not perfect, but neither am I."

"Yes, you are. In all the ways that matter, you are."

I push my glasses up on my nose. "I was lonely before Shane asked me out, Bash. My best friend lives in London and I'm not exactly a social butterfly. Now I have someone, and it's nice."

His brown eyes are locked onto me. I think of the lovesick teenage me who wanted nothing more than this—his undivided attention. Even if it wasn't the kind of attention I really wanted from him.

"It shouldn't be nice, though." His low voice has a hint of gravel. "It should take your breath away. Take over your life. Make you question your sanity."

I force myself to swallow, my heart pounding as I hold his gaze. "It's not like that for some people."

"Not for people who settle. And I don't—"

The shrill ring of an alarm stops him. I look away, sorting through my bag to find my phone, which is sounding with my seven fifty a.m. *pulling out of the driveway on weekdays for the lab* alarm.

"I have to go."

I grab my bag and water bottle and leave, my breathing still erratic as I get into my car.

It's the Bash effect. He could recite a dictionary and I'd react this way. I'd die of mortification if anyone knew I still feel this way about him.

I take a deep breath as I fasten my seat belt, switching my mind into research mode. That's why I'm here. If my research keeps going the way it has been, it's going to open professional doors for me.

This is my life. My career. I can't get sidetracked by my childhood crush.

"Encouraging results so far, Miss Morris." Professor Tom Carr eyes me over the rim of his glasses. "Keep me apprised."

I nod. "Of course. Thanks for looking it over."

"Anytime. I wish I had more time to work with you on this, but filling in teaching these summer classes changed my plans."

Our plan was to work side by side in the lab for a full month, but then one of his colleagues was injured in a car accident and he unexpectedly had to teach three summer classes. So now I'm in charge of the project and he assigned two grad student interns to assist me.

"I think we're in a good place with it," I say. "We're actually a little bit ahead of schedule."

"Glad to hear it."

I stand up to leave his office, stopping when he says, "Before you go, are you available to sit in with my TA on September 1? My wife and I are traveling that day for a wedding."

It's all I can do not to jump up and down with excitement. I've idolized Professor Carr since I started reading about his research in high school. He's a trailblazer in studying the connections between the microbiome and mental health, and he's open about his passion for it. He has a daughter who has depression, and he wants to help her and everyone else who battles it.

"I'd be honored to do that, of course."

He smiles. "Excellent. I'd like you to lecture in all three classes that day and include an overview of your current project for the advanced microbiology course."

"Absolutely. Thanks for asking me."

He nods, cueing the end of the conversation. I take my phone from my pocket to text Claire, my best friend, to tell her my good news. She's in London, so there are lags in our communication, but we text daily.

I have a waiting text from Suki.

Suki: Hi! Reminder that it's fondue night! 6 pm, come dip all the things in melted cheese and chocolate with us.

I smile at my phone, texting her back that I'll be there. She's been so welcoming to me. At the cook-out, she did everything she could to smooth over the tension Bash caused.

And tomorrow night is trivia with the Smartinis. Without Suki and her friends inviting me into their group, I'd just be working late at the lab or doom-scrolling on my phone over takeout at Bash's house.

I know I'm quirky and nerdy. I've never been ashamed of who I am. It's unusual, though, for a group as clever and funny as Suki and her friends to get me the way they seem to. I wish I had friends like them back home in Columbus.

I'm going to soak up every minute with them I can this summer.

———

I CLOSE MY EYES, shamelessly moaning as I get my first taste of Harry's cheese fondue. It's creamy and slightly savory, pairing perfectly with the cube of toasted bread I dipped in it.

"That's life changing," I say.

Harry grins and puts his palms together beneath his chin, nodding. "Thank you, my dear."

Mara has a bowl of cheese fondue, her breads and meats submerged in the melted cheese. True to his trim body, Dex has a plate of raw veggies and just one chunk of bread with a little fondue on it.

That's what I should do, but I don't. Instead, I make a plate of roasted meats, veggies and fondue, with several more chunks of bread. It's a good thing I stopped to get two bottles of wine to bring over since I'm eating like I'm on death row awaiting execution.

"What's in the fondue?" I ask Harry.

"I use Gruyère and Swiss. There's also some butter, herbs and white wine."

I close my eyes as I take another bite. I'm not sure I've ever tasted anything so delicious.

"See why fondue night is the best night of the month?" Mara says.

"Mm-hmm." I'm chewing, so I don't give a full answer.

The girls are dipping strawberries and marshmallows in the chocolate fondue fountain, Darling the pig snuffling up at the kitchen island the fountains are sitting on. The youngest girl, Hallie, slips him a chunk of bread.

"So, how did the rest of Saturday go, Lainey?" Suki asks me.

I set my plate down and thank Dex for the glass of wine he passes me. "Not great. Shane left when we got back to Bash's when Bash said we had to sleep in separate rooms."

Mara gasps. "No, he did not."

"He did."

I fill Mara, Dex and Harry in on what happened at the cookout, Mara slapping a hand over her mouth when she cackles over Bash's "speck of dust" comment.

"I'm so sorry for laughing," she says.

I wave a hand. "It's fine. It is a tiny stone. I just don't care. A relationship isn't supposed to be about how much things cost."

"Totally agree," Harry says.

Dex wrinkles his nose, leaning his hip against the kitchen counter. "True...but it's also about how much of what someone has they're willing to share with you. If he's just starting out and doesn't have a lot of money, that's one thing."

I don't really know how much money Shane has. The pool business he and his brother own seems to be doing great, but I don't know how much of their profit they have to reinvest back into the business. I've never thought of asking.

"Well, I went out with that investment banker I've been talking to." Mara looks over her shoulder to make sure the girls can't hear. "I was hoping to get railed within an inch of my life because it's been seven months and thirteen days, but who's counting? We were having a drink and he went to the bathroom. I ended up going to the bathroom, too, which is the only way I was able to see him *asking another woman for her number* on the way back to our table."

My jaw drops with shock. "No."

"Mm-hmm, girl. It's hell out there."

"What'd you do?" Dex asks, biting into a carrot with a crunch.

"I told her I was on a date with him and then I dumped my drink in his lap and left."

Suki walks over to Mara and clinks her glass.

"What do you do for a living, Mara?" I ask.

"I'm an attorney."

She's telling me about her work when I get an all too familiar rumble in my stomach.

Shit. Shit, shit, *shit*. I knew better than to eat so much cheese fondue, but I was excited about the invite here and wanted Harry to know how much I liked his food.

And now irritable bowel syndrome has joined the conversation. I know my body well, and I have less than thirty minutes until my intestinal tract detonates.

I can't spend thirty minutes or more shitting my guts out in one of Suki's bathrooms. I'd rather end up at a gross gas station bathroom if I can't get back to Bash's house on time.

The next rumble in my stomach is stronger, sending a little shot of pain through my gut.

Shit! Literally—shit incoming. I have to get out of here. I casually take my phone from my bag and pretend to read a text.

"Oh, crap."

"What is it?" Suki asks.

"One of the research assistants at the lab forgot to do final checks." I lie. "We have to make sure everything is off that's supposed to be off and everything's on that's supposed to be on. He has another thing and can't get back there to do it, so I have to."

"Fuck that guy," Dex says. "Fire him immediately."

I force a smile, but inside I'm freaking out. There have been a few times when I was trying to make it to my home bathroom and I didn't get there in time. Bash knows I have IBS, but he's never seen me at my worst during a bad flare or a pants-shitting incident.

"I'm so sorry, I have to go." I stuff my phone into my bag, begging my intestinal tract to let me make it back to Bash's. "You guys were so nice to include me, and this has been amazing. I really hate to leave."

"No, don't worry about it," Suki says. "Go do your thing and come back."

Shit. That wasn't a well-thought-out excuse. I can't come back. It'll be a minimum of a few hours before this episode is over—maybe even longer.

"I might. It'll depend on how long it takes me to get everything done at the lab."

I practically run to the door, the gurgle gaining momentum. This is the absolute worst.

"See you!" I wave over my shoulder as I bolt for my Camry, parked in front of the house. "Thanks!"

I start the car up and stomp on the gas pedal, my tires squealing as I peel out.

Please, Intestinal Gods, let me make it to Bash's house in time. I won't eat cheese for the rest of my life if I can just make it there on time.

CHAPTER SEVEN

Bash

"Put your arm around my shoulders, fuckstick."

Carter shoots a death glare my way. "I'm fine. Just get out of my way."

I wave my hand at the wide-open space in front of him. "No one's stopping you. Since you're fine, might as well run."

Leo laughs from my other side. Isaac is already in Carter's garage, raiding the chest freezer for one of the M&M ice cream sandwiches he loves.

"Laugh it up, bastards," Carter grumbles as he limps toward the door that leads into his kitchen. "It could have happened to you, and I wouldn't be laughing."

"Yeah...no," Leo says. "I play pickleball all the time and I've never injured myself."

"I just twisted my ankle. It's not an injury," Carter snaps.

We're making light of it because we all know how stressed he really is. Any injury could keep us off the ice. Even though it's the offseason, our contracts forbid us from doing things like skydiving, mountain climbing and skiing anytime. Our teams have a lot riding on us staying healthy.

The four of us were playing pickleball. And even though we are too competitive, it's generally a safe activity. Carter just lunged a little too far to the side and his foot got caught in a weird way.

He went down like a ton of bricks. And of course, he wouldn't let us carry him to the car or call our team doctor. His right ankle is so swollen that Leo had to drive his SUV home.

Leo and I exchange a look as Carter approaches the step that leads into his house. Neither one of us has to say anything. I cut in front of Carter to open the door and Leo takes his back.

Once I'm inside, I face Carter and bend my knees, offering him my arm to grab for support.

Leo's got more brute strength than anyone I've ever known. He ducks down and forces Carter to put an arm around his shoulder to help take the weight off his ankle.

The savory smell of grilled beef fills the air. That's right—it's fondue night. Once we get Carter into a chair, I'm going to dive face-first into that cheese fountain.

"Take it slowly," I say.

"Jesus, you two are like fussy old women," he gripes.

"What's going on?" Suki asks from behind me.

"He got into a fight with a little girl and she kicked his ass," I say. "She's probably still laughing over how hard he went down when she punched him."

"Bash, seriously. What's wrong with my husband?"

I let out a short bark of laughter. "So many things, Suki."

Carter, inside the house now, smacks away the arm I'm offering him, his brows lowered in a scowl. "I tripped playing pickleball and twisted my ankle. I'm fine."

"Did he say *pickleball?*" Dex asks from the living room.

Suki gasps. "You are *not* fine. Look how swollen your ankle is. Why are you walking on it?"

"Because I'm—"

"Leo, can you carry him to the couch?" she asks.

"Sure."

Carter bares his teeth like a rabid animal. Jesus fuck. The dramatics.

"You're not carrying me anywhere. Both of you take one side and I'll hop on one foot."

"I'll get ice," Suki says.

Leo and I shoulder Carter's weight. Even hopping makes him inhale sharply and hold his breath, which he only does when he's really hurting.

Dex and Harry clear decorative pillows off the sectional where they were sitting with Darling.

Darling is taking up almost half of the longest row of seats, his legs in the air and his little wanger peeking out from beneath his tight T-shirt.

"Off the couch, Darling," Carter barks as he approaches.

Darling looks up and yawns. He has Goldfish crumbs on his snout and doesn't give a single fuck about moving.

"Darling, come on," Mara says.

"Offer to sleep with him," Leo quips. "He's probably better looking than most of your boyfriends, right?"

"Says the guy who's so desperate he creeps on women in bathrooms."

"I wasn't creeping. I didn't even know you were in there."

"There's this revolutionary thing called knocking. Have you heard of it?"

Carter groans as we lower him to sit on the couch. "If you two don't stop, I'm gonna make you wear the same T-shirt until you're besties."

Mara blanches. "Matching T-shirts? How will that—"

Suki cuts in. "No, literally, the same T-shirt. He made Olivia and Charlotte share one of his T-shirts for two full days last week because they wouldn't stop fighting."

"It's what my mom did with me and my sister," Carter says. "It works."

Suki helps Carter get settled, putting pillows behind his back and ice on his ankle.

"Guys, please eat," Harry says. "We made so much food and all of us and the girls already ate."

My stomach growls in response to the invitation.

"Thanks, man. And remember what I told you about booking all of us for dinner at a nice restaurant soon. You guys feed me so much, I want to take a turn."

"Pick a place with top-shelf booze," Carter calls from the couch. "I'm getting my money's worth out of him."

I grab a plate and immediately remember my conversation with Lainey this morning in my kitchen. She looked so proper in her charcoal pants and black shirt, her hair back in a neat bun.

I'm not proud of how much time I spent during our conversation fantasizing about slowly unbuttoning that shirt, watching her eyes widen and her cheeks flush as I saw her tits for the first time.

"I forgot to invite Lainey." I set my plate back down, planning to text her.

"I invited her," Suki says. "She was here earlier, but she had to leave in a hurry because of something at the lab."

I check the time on my phone, concerned. It's 6:47 p.m. The campus will be dark soon and I don't like the thought of Lainey there all alone.

I text her.

Bash: Hey, where are you?

Lainey: Home. Why?

That's weird. I think she really likes Suki and her

friends, so why would she leave and lie about where she was going?

Then I see Leo raising a chunk of bread dripping with cheese fondue up to his mouth.

"Did she eat before she left?" I ask.

"Yeah," Suki says. "She really liked the fondue. I told her to come back when she's done, but she said it depends on how long it takes her."

I text Lainey again.

Bash: Are you going over for fondue night?

Lainey: I did earlier, but I had to leave. I'm sick. Please don't tell anyone.

I tuck my phone into my shorts pocket. "I have to go, guys."

Leo scrunches his face, confused. "What? Why?"

"Because he smelled you," Mara deadpans.

He scoffs. "That rotten fish smell ain't me, honey. It's that ecosystem in your overgrown bush."

I cut in. "I need to go check on Lainey. I think she might not be feeling well."

"Oh no," Suki says. "Do you need medicine? I have an entire pharmacy in our linen closet."

"Nah, but thanks."

I walk into the kitchen to leave through the door in there, and Isaac waves at me from the table. He has a plate in front of him loaded up with meats, vegetables and breads covered in cheese fondue and a second plate loaded up with fruit covered in chocolate fondue.

"First time eating?" I arch a brow at him.

He gives me a thumbs-up, his mouth stuffed full of food.

"See you, guys," I call over my shoulder.

"Hey, let me know how Lainey is," Suki says.

"I will."

I open the door and hear Dex say, "Carter, are you hungry? I can make you a plate."

"Thanks, man. My wife is oblivious to my starvation, as you can see."

I close the door, missing Suki's comeback to that one.

When I get out to my car, I text Lainey to ask if she needs anything.

Lainey: I'm okay. You don't need to leave because of me.

I've got my shortcomings, but I'm not going to stuff my face while she's sick. I have enough groceries at home to whip something up to eat later.

When I get home, Bruce greets me with his usual tail wag. I give him some love and a treat before heading upstairs to check on Lainey.

The door to her bedroom is wide open, but the bathroom door is closed.

"Hey, Lane," I call from the middle of the bedroom. "I'm home. You okay?"

"Yeah, I'm fine. I told you not to leave."

She doesn't sound fine. She sounds miserable.

"What can I do?"

"Nothing."

I furrow my brow, not liking her answer. Eric has told me how much she suffers with her IBS sometimes, and I hate not being able to do anything to help.

"You sure? I could make you something to eat."

She groans. "I can't eat, Bash. I'm fine, really."

I frown, looking at the pile of clothes on the chair in the corner. "You need me to do some laundry?"

"I didn't shit myself if that's what you mean," she snaps.

Fuck. I didn't think about that before I said it. "No, I just saw the pile of clothes in here. There has to be something I can do."

"There isn't. I just need to be alone."

I run a hand through my hair, knowing I should walk away. I can't seem to make myself do it, though.

"Are you in pain?"

"Bash, *leave*. I've been through this a thousand times."

Folding my hands on top of my head, I push down the helplessness. "I've got my phone. Call or text if you need me."

"I won't."

"Are you still pissed at me?"

"No! I just want you to get the fuck out of here!"

"I'm going," I grumble.

I go over to the chair and pick up the pile of dirty clothes. I can't just not do anything. Besides, who minds having their laundry done for them?

A skimpy pair of black satin undies slips out of the pile. As I pick them up, I imagine Lainey wearing them. The contrast of the dark fabric with her milky skin has to be sexy as fuck.

I wonder if she has a matching bra?

Shaking off the mental image that conjures, I take the laundry and leave the room. I'm supposed to be helping her, not sniffing her panties like a fucking creep.

Not that I did sniff her panties. And not that I'm thinking about it. I'm just washing her clothes, like the good friend I am.

CHAPTER EIGHT

Lainey

By the time my surprise colon cleanse is over, I'm tired and thirsty. I always am.

From the toilet, I posted in my online IBS support group about what happened, dubbing it "the fon-doo-doo incident." Several people told me they've been there. Only people who have IBS really understand how awful it can be. The memes and funny stories in the group always make me feel better when I'm down about it.

I like a meme in the group about spraying air freshener post-dump and making your bathroom smell like shitrus, then close out the app. I've already washed my hands and left the bathroom—I was just lying down for a few minutes before heading back downstairs for some water.

"Hey." Bash stands up from the couch. "You okay?"

I'm not used to someone being so concerned about me. When I tell Shane I'm having a flare, he leaves me alone and waits for me to get in touch with him when I'm myself again. Sometimes that takes days, but usually it's just a few hours.

"Yeah, I'm fine. I knew better than to eat that fondue."

"Who can resist a cheese fountain, though?"

I chuckle. "Clearly not me. Suki and her friends must think I'm insane. I made up an excuse about turning things off at the lab."

"They won't think anything of it. There's some stuff in the kitchen for you."

I furrow my brow because I wasn't expecting any deliveries. When I get into the kitchen, my eyes widen as I take in the things lined up on the island.

There's a case of Sprite, a case of 7-Up, a bottle of Pepto-Bismol, a box of Imodium tablets, bath salts, bubble bath, a six-pack of Gatorade, a bunch of bananas, a bag of brown rice and a container of probiotic supplements.

When I turn around, Bash is leaning against the kitchen counter, giving me a sheepish look.

"I Googled what might be good for you and Door Dashed it. It's okay if you don't want any of it."

I open my mouth to say something but close it again. I can't believe how open he's being about my condition. Most people find it uncomfortable to talk about uncontrollable shitting.

"You didn't have to do that," I say softly.

"I did it because I wanted to. I read that lean proteins and rice are a good meal after a flare, so I'll whip that up whenever you get hungry."

Tears fill my eyes and I turn away, hoping he didn't see. I spent all day replaying him calling me *perfect in all the ways that matter*. And the way he described what love should be...something that *takes your breath away, takes over your life and makes you question your sanity*—is going to live rent-free in my head forever.

I should still be pissed at him over the way he treated Shane, but instead, I'm swooning like a lovesick teenager. He's making me feel like my IBS isn't shameful. He looked up ways to help me.

"That's really nice, thank you." I open the case of 7-Up, not letting myself look at him. "I think I'll just have some of this for now."

The song his dryer plays when its cycle is finished sounds out from the laundry room, which is off the kitchen. He leaves to get the clothes, and I use the opportunity to get myself together.

Shane doesn't want to talk about my IBS because I've never talked to him about it. He leaves me alone because that's what I asked for. I should appreciate it. I *do* appreciate it. But it's hard not to compare him ignoring me when I have a flare to the way Bash is treating me now.

There's no reason to compare them, though. I knew who Bash was when I made a play for him seven years ago, and he turned me down. I started dating Shane because I became a realist. He's not perfect, but that's okay. He looks at me and sees a woman, and Bash looks at me and sees his best friend's kid sister.

Bash carries a small pile of laundry into the kitchen and sets it on the table.

"We can watch a movie if you want," he says as he starts folding clothes.

I do a double take when I see the women's black satin underwear on top of the pile. *My* underwear.

"You're doing my laundry." It comes out as an accusation.

"Yeah. Go pick out a movie."

He shakes one of my T-shirts and takes his time folding it carefully. It's weird to see him doing it, but I'm too worn out to argue with him. My laundry is done, and I'm just going to take the win.

I sit down on the leather sectional, Bruce jumping up beside me. He gets comfy while I turn on the TV and select Netflix.

His profile icon is Dwight from *The Office*, one of my favorite shows. I'm about to call into the kitchen and compliment him, but...

My heart sinks as I scan through Bash's recently watched shows and recommendations. *The Bachelor. Bridgerton. The Crown. Outlander.*

He has a girlfriend. There's no way he watched these shows. When he's home for holidays and visiting my parents' house, he and Eric only watch ESPN and whatever football games are on.

Is his girlfriend not here right now because I'm here? Guilt washes over me as I imagine Bash telling his girlfriend she can't Netflix and chill while he has a houseguest.

I'm cockblocking him. And also her.

"Hey." He sits down beside me, on the opposite side of Bruce. "See anything that looks good?"

"Do you have a girlfriend?"

He looks taken aback. "No, why?"

I tilt my head, giving him a look. "Don't bullshit me. You know I'm over my childhood infatuation with you. It's totally fine if you have a girlfriend, and you don't need to tell her she can't come over because of me. I have earplugs."

His brows shoot up in amusement. "I don't have a girlfriend. I'm not bullshitting you."

I frown. "Oh. Recent breakup?"

He shakes his head. "I'm not a relationship guy. Unless Bruce counts."

Hearing his name, Bruce jumps down from the couch and goes over to Bash, putting his front paws in Bash's lap. His tail swishes eagerly.

"Yeah, you're my one and only relationship, Brucey," Bash croons, cupping his dog's face.

I look from Bash to the TV screen and then back to Bash again. "What's up with your Netflix profile, then?"

He looks at the TV and shrugs. "I like shows that relax me."

My lips part and a laugh slips out. "*Bridgerton?* You like *Bridgerton?*"

"I'm team Kanthony. Have you watched it?"

I thought I knew Bash well. But this doesn't just surprise me; it shocks the hell out of me.

"It's one of my favorite shows. The spinoff, *Queen*

Charlotte, is perfection."

"You want to watch it?"

I glance from the TV screen to him, grinning. "It looks like you have *The Bachelor* in progress."

"You watch it?"

"No. But I can ask you questions and make you miss most of it because you're so busy explaining things to me."

"Let's do it."

Shane refuses to watch shows with me because I ask too many questions. Which is okay because we have very different tastes in shows. He likes action movies and I like quirky comedies and reality shows.

Bruce gets on the couch, half on Bash's lap and half on mine. Bash reaches behind my head and gets a blanket from the back of the couch, spreading it out to cover Bruce up.

"Has Shane called you since he left Saturday?"

I'm immediately defensive, but I try not to show it. "Yeah, we've talked. He's okay, but for the rest of the summer, he wants me to come to Columbus on weekends instead of him coming here."

Bash shakes his head. "And how do you feel about that?"

"I get it. He doesn't feel welcome here."

My heart is beating faster than its baseline. I'm

not used to being so close to Bash. He took a shower while I was sequestered in my room's bathroom. His dark hair is still damp, curling at the ends. And his lashes are just unfair. Dark and thick, framing caramel eyes with gold flecks.

"Tell me something, Lane." He rubs a hand over Bruce's back, his gaze intense as he looks into my eyes. "And be honest. I promise I won't say a word after if you'll just answer one question for me."

I should have a quip cued up, but all I can do is nod. I run my thumb over my engagement ring, feeling guilty over the warmth I feel from being so close to Bash.

"Does Shane make you feel like the most beautiful, sexy woman in the world? Like no one else could ever compare to you. Like he's all in, out of his mind, head over heels in love with you."

I swallow and look down. "Bash, it's not like that in real life."

He puts a fingertip beneath my chin and tips it up until our eyes meet. His touch makes my skin heat and my pulse pound. "It can be, though. It should. You're settling."

"Maybe," I concede. "But some of us don't want fireworks and passion. We don't want to land the hottest person we can and worry constantly about whether we'll be able to keep them as we get older. We just want stability and companionship."

He drops his hand. "Stability and companionship? That's like a commercial for a nursing home. Fuck that. You're a beautiful, brilliant twenty-four-year-old. You deserve nothing less than fireworks and passion. I've got married friends who have it all —they're best friends who can't keep their hands off each other."

I tuck a loose section of hair behind my ear, his words reaching me in a way that makes me uncomfortable.

"Just tell me you'll think about it," he says. "That's all I ask. This is me being completely serious. It's not really about Shane; it's about you and what you deserve."

"Okay. I'll think about it."

He sighs heavily, looking aggrieved. "If you want me to apologize to Shane, I will. You shouldn't have to drive to Columbus every weekend all summer in a car with no air conditioning."

I smile, surprised he humbled himself enough to even offer. "It won't be every weekend. He has to work a lot of weekends in the summer and he has video game tournaments sometimes."

Pursing his lips, he slides Bruce off his lap and gets up from the couch. "Just a sec."

He walks over to a chair with a decorative pillow on it. Adjusting the pillow so it's flat on the chair's seat, he then bends with one hand on the arm of the chair.

His arm muscles cord as he drives his fist into the pillow—hard—about half a dozen times. I'm surprised the pillow doesn't burst open. Bruce watches him, unfazed.

What the hell is he doing?

He stands upright, takes a deep breath in and out, and comes back to the couch. Standing with his hands on his hips, he says, "Sorry, I just had to get that energy out."

"Okay, but...why?"

"You. Are. Settling." He pinches the bridge of his nose. "And as someone who cares about you, it's painful to watch. I don't want you to end up miserable."

"Bash—"

"If you were my girl, and we were two and a half hours apart in the summer, you can bet your ass I'd be on your doorstep by seven thirty every Friday night, and I'd be getting up before sunrise to get back to work on Monday morning so I could have an extra night with you. If he wanted to, he would, Lane. And Shane doesn't want to."

If you were my girl. I can't even take a full breath as I replay his words in my head. Why? Why would Bash say something so thoughtless and cruel to me? He doesn't mean it. He's tearing down Shane, an average, everyday man, and making himself out to be the ten I could have if I only dumped Shane.

It's not realistic. And it hurts. It really, truly hurts my heart that he thinks it's okay to toy with my feelings this way. He wants me to dump Shane and be alone just so he can feel like he is right.

I clear my throat, pulling out my ponytail holder so I can hide my face behind a curtain of hair. Bruce jumps down from my lap as I start to stand up.

"You know what, my stomach's bothering me again."

Bash sighs heavily. "Lane, don't go."

"I need to. I think I just need to rest."

I rush up to my room, relieved when I finally close the door behind me. Just in case he comes up to see if I was lying, I go into the bathroom and close and lock the door.

I'll take a bath. Maybe it'll relax me a little bit. I'm not pissed off this time. I'm just so hurt I can hardly keep from crumpling up on the floor to cry my eyes out.

This is where I have to live for the summer, but it doesn't mean I have to spend much time here. I'm going to try just sleeping here and avoiding Bash because anytime we talk for more than five minutes, we end up arguing.

I've already had enough stress to last the entire summer.

CHAPTER NINE

Bash

HOW THE HELL is it only two thirty p.m.? I got an early start today, meeting up with Isaac for breakfast and then training with Carter and Leo. Then I had to get some photos taken and short videos shot by the Comets' PR people.

They're trying to keep fans engaged by following players in the offseason and checking in with short videos about what we're up to. They came to my house and took some videos of me and Bruce and I told them about my offseason training.

I didn't mention that I have a raging hard-on

most days or that my roommate might drive me over the edge before the next season starts. Figured those things aren't great for the team's image.

Lainey has been avoiding me for six days—since our conversation on the couch. She breezes past me in the kitchen every morning, refuses to make eye contact, and gives me a perfunctory wave after grabbing her water bottle. If I ask her questions, she tells me she's in a huge hurry.

Lie. She comes in late most evenings with a bag of ultraprocessed carryout in hand, bypassing the healthy meals I prepare. I feel like a fucking scorned housewife, standing there by the meal I worked to make, or at least heating up if my chef made it, and being ignored. All I need is an apron and some dishpan hands.

The texts I send her are glossed over; most of her responses include the word fine. It's fine. She's fine. Just busy. All good.

Bullshit. I asked her to carve out an hour for me this weekend so we could talk, and she said she couldn't because she's having an all-weekend sleepover with Mara and Suki at Mara's apartment.

Which leaves me home alone with Bruce. I came so close to texting Andi, the nurse I hook up with from time to time. She has been clear from the start that she doesn't want a relationship or feelings, which makes her perfect for me. When I go over to her place, we get right to it and then I leave.

I had my phone in hand, but for some reason, I couldn't do it. I'm a tightly wound ball of sexual frustration, yeah, but being on the outs with Lainey is killing me. She's meant to have a bright smile on her face, not a closed-off expression of resignation.

I'm also pissed as fuck at Shane. How fucking dare that douchebag play video games on weekends instead of coming to see Lainey? Cleveland is a blast in the summer. There are food festivals, concerts and farmers' markets.

Bruce is sitting by the treat jar, his not-so-subtle way of asking for one. I take out a couple and give them to him, scratching his ears. Maybe I'll take him for a hike. He'd like that.

When I start training camp, my full-time dog sitter, River, will move into the guesthouse in my backyard. He's a hippie nomad who backpacks during my offseason. He walks Bruce three times a day. And I pay him well for it.

I should walk him more in the summer. Poor dude probably dreams about River when he's gone.

"Okay, Bruce. Daddy's gotta take care of a little business and then we'll do something you'll like. I can't say the word because you'll go apeshit, but it starts with a *W*. Cool?"

He swishes his tail back and forth.

I leave him in the kitchen and go upstairs with my phone. I can't handle my perpetual erection any longer. I had to wear a cup during filming earlier to keep my dick locked down.

Stormi will be able to help me resolve this.

————————

MY TEAMMATE LUCIEN first introduced me to Stormi, a content creator with a massive following who calls herself a "meateorologist."

We all make fun of Lucien's fixation on Stormi because he's open about being a premium paid member of her site who beats off to her videos daily. He said he liked to hammer on it every morning in high school by watching a hot local weather forecaster, so Stormi is his dream woman.

She gives fake weather forecasts that always end with her getting herself off. They're mostly funny to me, but I'm in a desperate state here, and I won't be laughing today.

I go into my bathroom, grab a few tissues, and drop my shorts and underwear.

When I start her latest video, she appears on screen in a tight, hot-pink blazer and skirt, with nothing on beneath the blazer. The one button it has is fighting for its life as her massive tits stretch the fabric. Her long hair is loose around her shoulders and she's wearing dark-rimmed glasses.

"Thanks, Tom. Stormi St. James here with today's forecast." Her voice is breathy, her plump lips painted bright red. "It's going to be hot today. So very, very hot."

I lean my phone on a cologne bottle on my bathroom counter and wrap my palm around my dick. I'm not looking for anything elaborate—I just need to get off.

Stormi points at a weather map on a giant screen, the outline of a storm drawn over it shaped like a massive boner.

"Hold on to your headboards, ladies, because tropical storm Dick is bearing down *hard*. It's going to give us such a pounding." She slides a finger down one of her breasts, pulling her blazer open. "Oh. The forecast for the next hour is wet. It's soaking wet."

She cups her breasts in her hands, pushing them together. I stroke myself, an uninvited thought of

Lainey doing this to her breasts popping into my head and making me punch my brows together.

What the fuck? Stormi is the opposite of sweet, brilliant Lainey. I'm a bastard for picturing that.

She does have really nice tits, though. Round *C* cups that look damn good in a T-shirt.

Stormi pulls her skirt up a few inches, spreading her feet farther apart. "Oh my God. We're going to get six to nine inches. Six to nine desperately needed inches."

I close my eyes and picture Lainey curled up in bed, wearing a modest short-sleeved T-shirt and shorts. Lightweight, white fabric. I sneak into her room and curl up behind her, my erection pressing against her ass. She wakes up with a start but then snuggles back against me, telling me how good I feel.

"Dick is going to make us so wet. Absolutely soaked." Stormi pulls her skirt up farther, revealing her bare pussy.

I'm imagining myself sliding my hand down the front of Lainey's sleep shorts. She gasps as I stroke the soft curls between her thighs, telling her how much I love her sweet pussy.

"Oh God. This storm swell is like nothing I've ever seen." Stormi spreads her pussy lips to display her enormous clit.

I look down at the counter, envisioning Lainey flipping onto her back. I unbutton her sleep shirt and she tries to cover herself, but I hold her wrists above her head and suck on her nipples. Her moans make my dick throb, my balls aching with the need to feel her pussy clenching around me.

"Yes, Dick!" Stormi cries. "Give me a good pounding. I'm so wet and ready."

Though I can hear her, my mind is elsewhere. I'm sliding Lainey's sleep shorts off. I get on my knees, spreading her thighs apart. When I use the head of my cock to stroke up and down her slit, she moans my name, her soaked pussy begging to be fucked.

I thrust myself all the way in and she cries out, burying her nails in my shoulders.

"Yes! Give it to me, Dick!"

It's Lainey's voice I'm imagining, saying my name and rocking her hips up to take me deeper. Her cheeks are flushed and her expression is pure bliss.

I get the tissues positioned just in time, coming hard. I exhale heavily, glancing at my reflection in the mirror.

Fucking hell. The same brown eyes I'm used to are looking back at me. The two days' worth of dark stubble I was expecting. Hair messed up, a couple pieces falling onto my forehead.

But this isn't the man I thought I was. It's someone different. A man who just beat off while thinking about sweet Delaney Morris.

She was the girl who bedazzled her hula hoop and begged Eric and me to time her as she spun it around her hips in their backyard. The girl who ran lemonade stands to raise money for the animal shelter. The girl who begged me to take her to her senior prom seven years ago, tears shining in her eyes.

But now she's someone else to me. Someone more. She's the woman I'm...

I shake my head and look up at the ceiling. I'm done lying to myself. I'm not just attracted to her. It's more.

I want Lainey. All to myself. I don't want Shane to touch her ever again.

What the fuck? How much of a dumbass am I that masturbating to Stormi, the meateorologist, is what it took for me to figure this out?

Carter and Leo have been trying to tell me this for a while now. Carter's been beating me over the head with it, actually.

I don't know what the hell I'm going to do. This complicates everything.

I used to be someone Lainey wanted, but did I miss my chance with her? And, more importantly, can I be the man she needs? Can I commit myself to her, and only her, forever?

I'd never give her less than everything. She means too much to me.

Fuck. I hate having to tell Carter he was right.

CHAPTER TEN

Lainey

IT's day eight of the Great Bash Freeze-Out. And for a person who has a really hard time being mean to anyone, I'm doing pretty damn well.

I ambivalently sailed past the savory-smelling platter of freshly cooked bacon in the kitchen yesterday morning, my stomach begging me to give in. But no. Bash isn't winning me over with a delicious homemade breakfast. Those cinnamon rolls looked incredible, though. He probably had to throw them away since he's eating healthy to prepare for camp starting in two weeks.

When he texts asking if we can talk, I tell him I'm

busy. I was at Mara's from after work Friday night until Sunday afternoon when I had to come back to Bash's to work on my lectures for Professor Carr's classes. I went straight to my room and only came out to make a sandwich in the evening.

The craziest part is that I'm not even really mad at him anymore. I'm avoiding him because I'm not in a good place emotionally to talk to him.

I've been thinking about the things he asked me to consider. I only dated one guy before Shane, and that was a six-month college relationship that fizzled when he graduated. But even without much experience, I know Shane is definitely not head over heels in love with me. He's never called me *beautiful* or *sexy*.

Shane has been more of a comfortable presence in my life the past couple of years. We don't have a lot of sex, but when we do, it's...good for him every time and *good enough* for me, maybe half the time.

I wanted Shane to want to see me last weekend. But when I told him Mara and Suki invited me to have a sleepover, he wasn't disappointed. He said he had work to do and we could see each other another time.

I'm a scientist. I like logic and order. I used to be a starry-eyed romantic, but Bash broke me of that. I made a fool of myself to him and his rejection gutted me.

I promised myself I'd never feel that way again. I'd never fall so hard for someone that they had that kind of power over me. But maybe I went too far to the other end of the spectrum with Shane.

I once heard him tell his friends over his video game headset that he had time for another round of their game because I "probably had the shits." He laughed. My cheeks blazed with humiliation. He probably thought I couldn't hear him, but I was in his bedroom getting out the lingerie I'd packed for my first overnight stay at his house.

His thoughtless comment made me pack my bag up and tell him I wasn't feeling well, and that's when I decided we'd never spend an entire night together. He shrugged and waved at me over his shoulder, still playing his game.

It bothers me that he never fights for me. If we see each other, it's fine, and if we don't, that's fine, too. If we have an argument, he leaves, and he doesn't want to finish it later.

Bash drives me crazy with his nonstop criticism of Shane, but he's stubborn as fuck and I don't think he'll ever give up. He's a fighter.

I have to freeze him out because if I don't, I'm

going to fall for him again. Seventeen-year-old-me would never forgive me if that happened.

"Welcome to Harvest Moon," the greeter at Harry's restaurant says with a warm smile. "Can I get the name for your reservation?"

"I'm actually here to see Harry."

"Oh! Let me go grab him."

She's beautiful, her light-brown skin glowy and her thick, tightly-coiled curls bouncy. Her perfectly pressed bright-white dress shirt matches her teeth.

Harry asked me to come by to check out his restaurant before trivia night. I knew it would be incredible, but it's even more than I was expecting. The tables and floors are dark wood, the walls textured to look like soft brown saw grass. Candles in glass globes glow on every table and minimalist sconces and chandeliers provide a warm glow, but the overall vibe is dark and cozy.

"Lainey." Harry opens his arms as he approaches me. "I'm so glad you could come by."

He's wearing khakis and a light-blue polo, his short, dark-blond hair styled perfectly. Harry always looks put together and polished.

But me? I'm wearing jeans, Converse, and a well-worn black T-shirt that says, "Science doesn't care about your opinion." I changed out of my work clothes because dress shoes with pointy toes are bullshit.

"I'm finishing up a meeting in the kitchen," Harry says as he leads me to a table for two. "Give me one minute and I'll be back."

"Sure, take your time."

He wasn't kidding— he's back in less than two minutes, two glasses of something cloudy and light pink in hand.

"Hibiscus lemonade," he says. "I remember you saying you love lemonade, and this stuff is phenomenal."

I take a sip, then immediately have another. "That's amazing. It's sweet and tart at the same time. There's like a cranberry flavor."

"I'm obsessed. I drink about a half gallon a day."

It's around four thirty p.m., and busy staffers are coming in and out of the double doors that lead to the kitchen. One bartender is polishing the gleaming bar surface and another is lining up clean glass tumblers.

"Is this the prep time before it gets crazy?" I ask.

"Pretty much, but it's nothing like Fridays and Saturdays. We seat people starting at four forty-five and we have a full house tonight."

The scent of seasoned, grilled meat makes my

stomach growl. I'm surprised when a server approaches our table and sets down a plate of dumplings, pinched perfectly and drizzled with a dark sauce.

"I'm having the kitchen bring us some snacks," Harry says.

"Wow." I look up at the server. "Thanks, this looks amazing."

She grins. "Enjoy. Anything else right now, boss man?"

"I think we're good." Harry picks up a small plate and passes it to me. "Dig in."

"This place is..." I shake my head. "I'm blown away, Harry. Seriously. You look like you're still in your twenties, and I could try my whole life to create someplace like this and never even come close."

"That's very kind, thank you. I'm thirty-two. And I don't remember if I told you I actually sold this place last year. Part of the deal was that I stay on as executive chef for two years."

I serve myself a dumpling, steam rising from it as I cut into it. "So what's your plan after that? Or have you even decided?"

"I'm opening another restaurant. The two years were to help transition, but also for noncompete reasons. I think my next one will be an Asian sushi, ramen, wood-fired pizza mashup."

"Oh, hell yeah. I'd be all over that."

"Right? I could live entirely on sushi."

My first bite of the dumpling makes me moan softly. It's divine—tender, perfectly seasoned beef, onions and carrots with a savory and sweet sauce. "That's orgasmic."

He smiles widely, pleased. "My sous came up with that recipe. It's a new one. She'll be thrilled you like it."

"Like it? I could eat about thirty-five of these."

He laughs. "I just love you. You remind me so much of Mara and Suki."

His compliment warms me. "Thank you. I adore all of you. Without you guys, I'd have nothing here but my work at the lab."

Harry is able to arch just one brow. I'd look ridiculous trying to do that.

"I mean, we'll take all your free time, but what about Bash? And your fiancé? He's not far away, right?"

I heave out a sigh. "It's kind of a situation."

"Is it something you want to talk about?"

"Sure, I don't mind."

"The rest of the Smartinis will be here by five for

our pregame drinks and snacks sesh. Do you want to wait and tell all of us at once?"

God, it would be nice to find out what they all think. I'm so tired of running over it in my head and never really figuring anything out. "Yeah, sure."

"You need a shot to loosen you up?"

I laugh because what an understatement. "Definitely."

———

"OH, HAYYYLLL NAW." Mara is about a drink and a half past tipsy. "Fuck that fucker. He spends seven grand on a gaming computer and you get *this* engagement ring?" She bends to inspect my ring closer. "Baby, I've got blackheads bigger than that diamond."

I've been telling the other Smartinis about Shane, starting with big-picture things like him never saying I look good or I'm beautiful. But as the night has gone on and the drinks have gone down, I've opened up and now I'm spilling my guts.

We're at The Factory, an old warehouse that was converted into a bar and restaurant. After taking first place in the weekly trivia on the bar side, we decided to stay and talk some more.

I look down at the ring that turned my finger green before I had it plated with rhodium by a jeweler to protect my skin.

"I said it didn't matter how much he spent, but..."

"We all say that," Suki says. "But for fuck's sake, none of us mean it. A ring you're going to wear for your entire life doesn't need to cost a fortune, but you want it to be pretty."

I blanch. "Are you saying my ring isn't pretty?"

Her eyes widen with alarm. "No, I...I didn't mean it like that."

I burst out laughing. "I'm fucking with you. This ring is ugly as shit."

The entire table erupts with laughter. I feel lighter and happier than I've felt in a long time. I didn't realize how much I needed real-life close friends to confide in.

"I'm getting the next round," Dex says, getting up from the table.

"He said the G-spot is a myth," I say. "But science has proven it's real."

Mara rolls her eyes and cackles. "My response to that horseshit is threefold: unicorns are a myth, the G-spot is super fucking real, and Shane sucks in bed."

Harry raises his glass. "Shane sucks in bed!"

Suki frowns. "Should we be toasting that, though? Lainey's engaged to him."

Harry frowns, burps, and then lowers his glass. "Right."

"I think it was a good call taking an Uber tonight," Suki says with a laugh.

"I'm going to need to talk to Shane about that," I say softly. "I think we should probably postpone the wedding."

Suki's expression turns serious. "Is that really what you want? We've been having fun talking shit, but I don't want you to do something you'll regret because of tonight."

I shake my head. "No, I've been thinking about this on my own for the past week. Bash told me Shane should be all in, crazy in love with me, or I'll be settling."

She softens. "Bash said that?"

"Yeah. He said Shane should be here every Friday night through Monday morning. That he would be —Bash, I mean."

Suki's brows fly up. "Wait a minute, Bash said what?"

There's a flutter in my stomach as I replay it in my head. "He said it I was his girl, and he lived in Columbus; he'd be here by seven thirty every Friday night. And he'd get up early every Monday to drive back so he could have an extra night."

Suki and Mara exchange a look. Harry covers my hand with his.

"After you have a talk with Shane, have a talk with Bash," he says.

Dex returns with a tray of drinks, passing them around. Mine is water because two drinks is my max on a weeknight.

"So, if you guys are up for the most embarrassing story ever—"

"Always!" Suki gives me a warm smile.

I take a deep breath. "Okay, so Bash was my brother Eric's childhood best friend, right? They were together all the time. Every day. I idolized both of them, but when I was in fifth grade, I developed a hardcore crush on Bash. I kissed my pillow, imagining it was him, all that stuff."

"Wait, how much older is he than you?" Dex asks.

"Four years. Every time he and Eric went to a dance with dates and they came over for my mom to take pictures, it broke my heart."

"Aw." Harry pats my hand.

"Yeah, and imagine me with even oranger hair, braces and bad skin. I was so awkward. But my hair got darker and finally, at the age of like fifteen, I got some boobs. So I was feeling better about myself, and when I was seventeen, I..." I blow out a breath. "I drove to his house and asked Bash to my prom."

"Oh God," Mara says.

"Exactly. He said no, of course. I cried and ran back to my car, planning to get the hell out of there, and it wouldn't start."

Dex claps a hand over his mouth.

"Oh, Lainey," Suki says.

"Yeah. Bash called my parents, which got me into the deepest of shit because I'd lied about where I was going. He drove me home, which took more than six hours. I've never been so mortified in my life. He was so nice, telling me I was a great girl and any guy my age would be lucky to have me..." I shake my head. "And then, to make it even worse, the next week, he got my car fixed and drove it back home. My parents made me write him a thank-you card."

They're all giving me sympathetic looks, Dex's face frozen in a cringe. Finally, Mara breaks the silence.

"That's awful. I'm sorry. I mean, not that he got your car fixed, but you know what I'm saying."

"Yeah. It took years for me to even be able to be around him again."

"On an entirely different subject," Mara says.

"Does anyone want to share nachos with me? With so much extra cheese sauce that we need a snorkel and flippers to get to the nachos."

"Hell yes," Suki says.

I pass, fondue night still fresh in my mind.

My phone, which is face down on the table, buzzes with a new text. I flip it over, expecting to see a message from Shane.

Bash: Hey, just checking on you because it's getting late. You ok?

It's weird that my fiancé hasn't texted me since yesterday, but Bash is concerned about me. It makes the voice of doubt about Shane in my head grow just a little louder.

CHAPTER ELEVEN

Bash

LAINEY HASN'T EVEN OPENED the box of frosted cherry Pop-Tarts in the pantry. Or the Junior Mints.

I look down at Bruce as I close the pantry door, shaking my head. "She's really pissed, dude. It might be time to break out some wieners."

Ballpark wieners, that is. Lainey's parents used to have a bonfire just about every weekend in the summer. She always loved roasting her own hot dogs in the flames, preferring them charred to a crisp.

I didn't even realize those were the good old days until they were over. Eric and I would set up a two-person tent and sleep in sleeping bags, sneaking out of it with flashlights to roam the neighborhood in the middle of the night.

He's an insurance agent now. Married with a two-year-old daughter and another kid on the way.

Lainey finally got home around twelve thirty this morning. I was on the couch waiting, and she barely even acknowledged me, as usual. My attraction to her has taken over my thoughts. Even though I know Lainey isn't a person who would cheat in a relationship, I fought my urge to ask her where she'd been.

Who even am I? She's not my girlfriend. I'm not even a jealous type. I've always told myself if a woman wants me, great. And if not, someone else will. And up until now, the more emotionally detached women were from me, the better.

It's all different with Lainey, though. She's not just a woman. I care for her. And her being mad at me for more than a week feels like someone's shredding my insides with a cheese grater.

Makes me want to kick my own ass, honestly. And that's as fucked up as I've ever been over anyone.

I'm home alone with Bruce in the middle of the day. My workouts are over and I've got an hour before I have to leave for my afternoon volunteering coaching youth hockey. I might need to ask those pimple-faced fourteen-year-olds for some advice on women.

He's probably busy, but what the hell. I push a button on my phone screen to call Eric.

"Sebastian Stone." He answers on the second ring, a smile in his tone. "How the hell are you?"

"Still sexy as fuck. How are you, brother?"

"No complaints. Callie's morning sickness passed, thank fuck. She wasn't just sick in the morning; it was all the time. Neither one of us was getting enough sleep for a couple of months."

"Damn. Glad she's feeling better. Is this a good time to talk?"

"Yeah, I'm on the way from lunch back to the office. What's new?"

I move the phone away from my mouth and huff out a sigh. Eric has known me for so long that I don't need to tiptoe.

"Lainey's pissed at me."

He barks out a single note of laughter. "She can be a hothead. She'll get over it."

"It's been more than a week. She won't look at me and she blows me off every time I text her or try to talk to her."

After a couple seconds of silence, he says, "Is she okay?"

"Yeah, I think so. She's gotten to know Carter's wife Suki and her friends and she went out to trivia with them last night. Didn't get home 'til twelve thirty."

He chuckles. "She's a grown-ass woman, man. She knows how to take care of herself."

I stand up from the recliner I'm sitting in, agitated. "It's not that she came home late, it's that she's pissed at me."

"What'd you do?"

I pause. How can I tell him what I said without making him assume it was just me dogging on Shane like I always do?

"Shane came to visit her first weekend here. I was a shit to him and he got pissed and left. He wouldn't even talk to Lainey; he just drove off. I don't like the way he treats her."

"Keep this between you and me, but my parents aren't thrilled with Shane, either."

I stop pacing. "Why?"

"Mom referred her friend Jenny to Shane's business because Jenny's daughter and her husband want to build a pool. Jenny's daughter didn't say anything about how she heard about his business, and she told her mom, who told my mom, that Shane made her uncomfortable when he came over to give her an estimate."

My pulse pounds, anger already building in his chest. "How? What did he do?"

Eric sighs heavily. "Something about him telling her he'd move them up on the schedule in order to get her into a bikini faster, as long as she'd sent him pics of her in it."

"That motherfucker."

"Exactly. I told Mom she needs to tell Lainey, but she's worried Lainey will just get mad at her."

My jaw tenses. "She excuses his shitty behavior. Just because it's not the worst possible shit a man could do to a woman, that doesn't make it okay."

"You know I agree." His voice is glum. "I feel bad. Like I ignored little warning signs because she was so happy."

"Like what?"

There's a pause. "He calls her a nerd. Not in an affectionate way. Callie has never liked him, and she hates him at this point because she and Lainey got ready for Shane and Lainey's engagement party, and Shane didn't say a thing about how Lainey looked when he saw her. He just said, 'Hey.'"

"What the fuck? Why are you just now telling me all this?"

He hums, considering. "I don't know. We just haven't talked in a while. Have we talked since the engagement party? I know I texted to make sure you were okay the next morning because you got so hammered."

That headache lasted two days.

"You should have called me." I run a hand through my hair, pacing into the kitchen. "I knew I should have punched that smug bastard when I had the chance."

"I guess I need to talk to Lainey," he says.

"Yeah, you do. Today."

"She's doing okay otherwise? Mom said her research thing's going well."

My jaw refuses to unclench. "I don't know because she hasn't talked to me in more than a week."

"Oh yeah, you never told me what you did."

"I told her Shane's not good enough for her."

A pause. "That's it?"

"Yep."

"You've said that to her a lot and she usually blows you off."

"Not this time. I think she might have cried."

He exhales hard. "Shit. Okay, I'll talk to her today."

"Let me know how it goes."

"Bash, I'm just pulling into the office, but is there something else going on with you? You sound different."

It's the worst possible time to tell him. Or is it the best? We're on the phone, so he can't punch me. And he has to go, so he can't yell at me for the next hour.

"I might have feelings for Lainey."

I hear him opening his car door, and then the other end of the line goes deathly silent. "Eric?"

"You *might*?" The car door closes again. Shit.

I square my shoulders. It's time to man up. "I do."

"What kind of feelings?"

My laugh is humorless. "You don't want me to go into detail, trust me."

"Jesus fuck, Bash. I have to tell my sister her fiancé is a piece of shit later today. If you fuck her when she's vulnerable, I'll never speak to you again."

I scowl. "What the hell kind of guy do you think I am? I'd never do that."

"You said *feelings*, which for you means one thing."

I shake my head, the truth really sinking in now that I'm saying it out loud. "Not this time."

"Bash." He's agitated. "I have a meeting. I can't talk about this right now. Are you sure? Because seriously, when you turned her down for prom, she was devastated. If she thinks there's a chance and then you fuck her over—"

"I was twenty-one and she was seventeen!" I yell. "If it got out I took a minor to her prom, the league would have put me out on my ass!"

"That wasn't the reason you said no, and we both know it."

My shoulders slump. "No, it wasn't. I didn't feel that way about her, and I don't even know where it came from, but since she moved in with me...I can't think about anything else."

He groans. "Have you said anything to her about it?"

"No. You're the only one I've told."

"Okay. I'll talk to her and I guess we'll see what she decides. But either way, keep it in your fucking pants."

"Don't be a dick."

"Don't *you* be a dick. That's my sister. I know you."

I want to throw my phone into the wall. I was already tied up in knots over Lainey, and now it feels like someone set the knots on fire.

"You think I'm such an asshole that I'd prey on Lainey? Use her? That's what you think?"

"No. You know I don't think that. I'm just saying give her time. That's reasonable, right?"

"Of course. But I don't need you telling me that. I already know. Give me some fucking credit. I'm the only one who's been saying all along that Shane's a fucking loser."

"I really have to go. Let's talk later."

"Okay. Text me to let me know how it goes with Lainey, okay?"

"I will."

I end the call and scrub a hand down my face. It's a good thing I'll be busy with youth hockey all afternoon. Any distraction from thinking about Eric and Lainey's conversation will help keep me from losing my mind over it.

CHAPTER TWELVE

Lainey

I'VE NEVER BEEN SO happy to be driving away from my hometown. The past hour was a complete shit show, and I just want to escape.

Earlier today, an average afternoon at the lab turned into a nightmare of a day when my brother called me. He told me about a comment Shane made to our mom's friend's daughter that literally turned my stomach.

Never once has Shane said I'm pretty or that I look good in an outfit. Tears ran down my cheeks when Eric told me Shane asked for photos of another woman in a bikini. While he was working. It's disgusting.

It wasn't just that one thing. Eric said he regrets not telling me Shane wasn't right for me a long time ago. He said he thought as long as I was happy, it wasn't for him to interfere. But apparently my sister-in-law Callie has disliked Shane all along and has been telling Eric he needed to say something.

I was embarrassed. Mortified. And really fucking angry. As soon as my shift at the lab was over, I drove straight to Columbus to confront Shane. He wasn't at home or his office, and he wasn't answering his phone.

I waited for him, and things took an ugly turn when he brought a woman home and found me sitting on his darkened front porch.

Our confrontation was short. I gave him back his piece-of-shit ring and told him to go fuck himself. I wish I could've been badass enough to be icy cool as I did it, but I sobbed the entire time.

I'm just ten minutes out from Bash's house and I'm still sobbing. I've been guzzling fountain Dr Peppers and eating my feelings. My feelings insisted that only drive-through burritos with extra sour cream would do, so I had to stop at a gas station to shit my guts out. While sobbing.

Fuck this day. And fuck Shane.

I was talking to a florist about wedding flowers earlier. Guess I can cross that off my to-do list.

Squaring my shoulders, I resolve not to cry even one more tear over that asshole.

"No more pretending I care about pool chemicals," I say to my empty car. "At least he's not getting laid tonight."

My laugh sounds maniacal. After returning Shane's ring, I was walking back to my car when I turned around and told his lady friend I hoped she enjoyed four-inch erections and premature ejaculation. She bowed her head and left.

I crank up "Enough for You" by Olivia Rodrigo, fresh tears springing to my eyes. Normally, I'm not so emotional, but right now, I'm so angry I can't even think straight. I was good to him, and he gave me the bare minimum.

He didn't even propose. When I told him I was applying for grad school in other states and would be moving if I got in, he asked me if I'd stay. When I said I'd only stay if we were engaged or married, he said we could consider ourselves engaged.

He handed me the ring that weekend. That was it. And I convinced myself that I had something great because it was the only thing I ever had.

Hopefully Bash isn't home. He'll take one look at my splotchy face and swollen eyes and demand I tell him everything. I'm wiped out in every possible way and all I want is to wash my face and crawl into bed.

The outside lights are on, but the inside of the house is darkened when I pull into the driveway. It's almost midnight. Bash should be in bed.

I type in the code on the keypad by the garage to raise the door, then close it with the button next to the door that leads inside.

When I walk inside, all I hear is the clack of Bruce's nails on the wood floor as he comes to greet me. I exhale softly, relieved. I could use some Bruce cuddles before bed.

I grab one of my water bottles from the fridge, planning to tiptoe past the living area to get upstairs.

But then the lights come on. Bash is standing next to the switch, his expression morphing from concern to sympathy when he sees me.

Tears spring to my eyes. Why can't I just be done crying?

"I don't want to talk about it." I stumble over the words, fighting a sob.

He walks toward me, opening his arms. I can't hold my feelings back any longer. The dam breaks as he wraps his arms around me, swallowing me up.

I don't realize how much I need it until I sink against his taut, broad chest. He doesn't say a word. He just holds me, his warmth steadying me. After about a minute, he lifts my feet up from the floor and carries me over to his massive sectional.

He sits down and settles me into his lap, my legs off to one side and his arms still wrapped tightly around my back.

It's kind of funny. The first time I had my heart broken by a man, Bash was the only one there in the immediate aftermath, and he tried his best to comfort me. Here we are again, only this time he wasn't the one who inflicted the pain, and he's doing exactly what I need most.

It's too raw for me to talk about. I'm exhausted. But I'm not alone, and that feels good. Bruce jumps up by my feet and curls up.

My cheek rests on his shoulder, and it's a hard pillow, but his pine-and-amber scent makes up for it. I cry some more, his arms tightening around me and his cheek resting on top of my head.

I've been giving him the silent treatment even though he didn't deserve it. But still, he's right here when I need him most. Bash really is a good friend.

My eyelids droop and I give in to the pull of sleep.

The smell of bacon wakes me up. I'm lying on the sectional, a blanket covering me and a pillow beneath my head.

I feel like I got run over. My head aches and my throat is dry. Last night comes back in a rush. I glance at the empty spot on my finger where my engagement ring was.

"Shit!" I fly up, tangling my limbs in the blanket. "What time is it?"

"Seven," Bash says from the kitchen, where he's cooking something at the stove. "I'm making breakfast in case you're planning to go into the lab."

I groan, because that sounds terrible. I don't have set hours, but I treat it like a job, even though I'm not getting paid. A strong recommendation from Professor Carr based on my performance this semester will open doors for me.

Standing up, I take a deep breath. "I have to go in, at least for the morning."

"How you feeling?"

I laugh lightly. "Like hot garbage."

"Have some juice. Breakfast is almost ready. We'll get you fixed up before you have to leave."

We. A wave of gratitude brings a lump to my

throat. I practically run into the kitchen and slide my arms around Bash's back in a hug.

"I'm sorry I was a dick to you." I press my cheek to his broad, muscled back.

He puts one of his much larger hands over mine against his chest. "It's okay, Lane."

I move to stand with my back against the counter so I can see his face. "Did Eric tell you?"

"About him calling you to talk about Shane? We talked before he did it."

My brows shoot up. "Wait. Did you tell him to tell me?"

He shrugs. "What matters is that you know."

My heart swells and aches at the same time. "You did. You knew this whole time and that's why you've been trying to convince me to leave him and have it be my idea."

He frowns. "Not exactly. I've never thought he was good enough for you."

I rub my forehead. "I have the most killer headache."

"Get some juice. Seriously. And there's Tylenol in one of the island drawers."

"I will." I run my hands through my hair, suddenly self-conscious. "Hey, how bad do my eyes look?"

He looks at me and then considers for a beat, making me laugh. "That good, huh?"

"They've looked better." He grins. "But you're still beautiful Brainy Lainey."

My heart does a little flip. "It was just Brainy Lainey, you know. You guys never called me beautiful."

"Be kind of weird for your own brother to say that about you, wouldn't it?"

His gaze on me is warm, but not in the usual way. I swear he's looking at my mouth. I can't let myself fall into my old, Bash-infatuated ways.

"I guess it would be weird for my brother's best friend, who thinks of me like a sister, to say it too," I quip.

Something flickers in his eyes and he turns back to the bacon. I push away from the counter.

"I need to go take a shower. Thanks for being such a good friend."

"Hey."

I turn to look at him.

"Have you called Shane yet?"

My former fiancé's stunned but not stricken expression when he got caught bringing a woman home flashes through my mind. He asked, "What are you doing here?" like I was the one who owed him an explanation and not the other way around.

"I went to Columbus last night. Shane and I are over."

Bash's expression lights up with happiness that he quickly masks. "Do you want to talk about it?"

"Later. I have to go into the lab for the morning, but if you'll be around this afternoon—"

"Yeah, of course. Can I take you out for lunch later?"

God, he's so damn nice. Next time I fall in love, I'm going to look for a man who's nice and also hot for me. If that combination even exists. There are more than four billion men in the world, so mathematically speaking, it should be possible.

"Yes, that would be nice. And then I'm going to make some sourdough bread. That's always therapeutic."

He nods approvingly. "I'll eat the fuck out of it."

I smile. "You don't have to. I know you have to watch your diet."

"I'm all over it, Lane. Better make two loaves."

"I feel like baking and cooking." The idea is just forming in my head. "Maybe we could have Suki and Carter and the whole crew over for dinner this weekend."

"Great idea. I'll help."

"Okay. I'll invite them."

I turn to go upstairs, glancing over my shoulder as I walk. Bash is watching me, that look back in his eyes that I can't quite place.

After he turned me down seven years ago, I never would have thought we'd end up being close friends like this. I've always felt like Bash was my friend as an offshoot to being Eric's friend, but this summer is bringing us a lot closer together.

Some woman is going to be incredibly lucky to snag him one day. And I doubt we'll ever get time to be such close friends as we are now once that happens. This is my chance for one-on-one time with Bash, and even though I spent years hoping for a romance with him, there's something solid and right about at least having him as one of my closest friends.

CHAPTER THIRTEEN

Bash

LAINEY TALKS TO HER DOUGH.

Actually, she talks to it in all stages. She keeps the starter in a jar in the fridge and knows by smelling it when Dough Goldberg is "happy" or "hungry." She's been obsessing over it for two days now, mumbling over fermentation, flour and proofing.

None of it means anything to me, but it's pretty fucking cute. Alarms sound on her phone every hour —if not more often—and she runs to check on her dough, stretch it and poke it. That dough is getting way more action than I am.

We had a weekend Netflix marathon so she could

stay close to the damn dough. I tried to get her to go out, but she refused. Now it's Sunday afternoon and my kitchen is messier than it's ever been as we work to make dinner for our friends.

The pasta sauce we made from scratch with tomatoes from the farmers' market is simmering, a splatter hitting me in the face as I push a button on my phone to answer the call that's coming in. I put it on speaker since my hands are occupied cooking.

"Hey, Mom."

"You actually answered."

I roll my eyes. "Sorry, I was busy the last couple of times you called."

"I understand. I'm nothing special, just the woman who spent twenty-three hours in labor pushing you out of her vagina."

Lainey meets my eyes and grins from the other side of the kitchen.

"So how are you, Mom?"

"Good, good. We had the church garage sale yesterday and I worked it from seven a.m. until five p.m. I'm still tired."

"I'm sure the Lord appreciates your efforts."

"Sebastian Patrick, don't joke about the holy father."

I gather a pile of chopped carrots into my hands

and move them from the cutting board into a bowl. Lainey wanted to include every vegetable that exists in this chopped salad, and she's working on two homemade dressings for it: buttermilk ranch and balsamic vinaigrette.

"Sorry, Ma," I say perfunctorily.

My parents are devout Catholics. I'm not, but I still go to church with them when I'm home for Easter and Christmas.

"What's this I hear about Lainey's fiancé breaking up with her? Is it true?"

I lock eyes with Lainey. She waves her hands and shakes her head, silently telling me not to mention to my mom that she's here and we're on speaker.

"Lainey was the one who broke up with him."

"Good. He has a look about him. I never trusted him. And he's already been seen out with another woman. Shameless."

I cringe, wishing Lainey didn't have to listen to this.

"Lainey and I are making dinner for some friends right now."

"You are?"

"Yep. Spaghetti, salad and Lainey's sourdough bread. With flourless chocolate cake for dessert."

She sniffs. "I guess our invitation to dinner got lost in the mail."

Lainey laughs silently.

"I'll invite you guys for dinner soon," I say.

"That's more like it. We're not that far away, you know. You could come home for a weekend."

"Yeah, I will."

"I heard you sigh. Why are you sighing?"

I shake my head. I love my mother, but sometimes I wish I wasn't an only child. I could use some siblings to spread her love out among them.

"I was sighing over the spaghetti sauce, Ma. It splattered me."

"Well, turn down the heat. You don't want it to scorch."

"I'll do that."

"Is Lainey there? Can I talk to her?"

I grin at Lainey, whose eyes are like saucers. She shakes her head adamantly.

"Let me see."

Lainey mouths, "no." She was raw the first couple of days after the breakup, but she's back to her usual self. I smirk at her.

"Yeah, she's right here."

Lainey glares at me as she walks over. "Hey, Mrs. Stone. How are you?"

"Lainey, how are you, honey? I'm sorry to hear about your breakup, but I think it's for the best."

"Thank you. I think so, too."

"Your mother already has grandbabies, so there's no pressure on you. Me? I may never have any, and I've come to accept that. All I get is my granddog."

I roll my eyes dramatically.

"Oh, don't say that, Mrs. Stone. Bash is great with his friends' daughters. You might still have a chance."

"He is? You think so?"

I shoot Lainey a scowl because now my mom will ride me relentlessly about when I'm going to settle down.

"Yeah, I think he just needs some encouragement," Lainey says.

I pick up the phone and take it off speaker. "Hey Mom, we have to go. Lots of work left to do on dinner."

"Okay, keep that heat turned down. And call me sometime so I know you haven't forgotten your parents exist. We used to wipe your butt, you know. Show some gratitude."

"I will, Ma. Love you."

"I love you, too."

I end the call and give Lainey a look. "What the hell was that?"

She shrugs. "You fucked around and found out. How did your mom hear about me and Shane breaking up?"

"Probably just neighborhood gossip. Maybe your mom told her."

"It's probably the only time anything gossip-worthy will happen to me," she quips.

She has her hair pulled up in a high ponytail, a loose strand resting against one of her rosy cheeks. I want to pick her up, set her on the kitchen counter and kiss the hell out of her. Find out just how pink those cheeks can get. Pull her body flush against mine.

"Can you keep an eye on things while I get a quick shower?" she asks.

My cock twitches with interest. I had to do another round of Stormi the Meateorologist last night before my balls exploded, but with the sound off since Lainey was upstairs. I couldn't get off until I stopped watching Stormi and started imagining sneaking into Lainey's room.

I fantasized about her waking up to find me getting into bed with her. She blushed and asked me what I wanted. I told her to be a good girl and undress for me. Just the thought of touching her pussy was enough to get me there.

When I lost my virginity, it was to a woman who was twenty-one. I was eighteen. I was so damn careful in high school, busting my ass to make it in hockey and unwilling to risk getting someone pregnant.

Every woman I've ever been with has been experienced. Bare pussies, sexy tats, sometimes even pierced nipples. I've always enjoyed women who know what they want in bed and aren't afraid to ask for it.

But Lainey's innocence is like a drug to me. I'm sure she's not a virgin, but she's shy. I imagine she's a passive participant, and Shane probably only did the bare minimum. Does she even know how mind-blowing sex can be?

In my fantasies, she has no idea. She gasps and blushes and presses her knees together. I'm so wound up wondering how she'd respond if I tried anything.

I can't, of course. Not when she's fresh off a breakup. But fuck, it's killing me to spend so much time with her and never touch her. Or worse, only touch her in a platonic way.

When she came home from Columbus that night, all I wanted was to fuck the hurt away. I'm not that guy, though. I ignored my urges and only offered her comfort.

"I got it," I tell her. "You want me to cut up the bread?"

Her eyes flash with alarm. "No! Don't touch it."

"What if I just fondle it a little bit?"

She laughs. "You're such a creep. Don't fondle my sourdough."

"Just some dirty talk?"

A light flush blooms on her cheeks. That's...encouraging.

"Have at it, as long as you're done when I get back in fifteen minutes."

She goes upstairs and I hear her turn on some music. She loves '80s songs. I'm just glad she's not curled up in a corner listening to "Everybody Hurts" by REM on repeat. She was so upset the night she broke it off with Shane I thought she might be down for a while.

Lainey's resilient, though. And brave. That time she showed up at my house to tell me she had feelings for me, I reacted the way an adult should act when a minor tells them that. I told her we couldn't get involved and I couldn't take her to her prom.

I admired her courage, though. When her parents suggested that maybe she become a science teacher instead of reaching for her own goal of getting a doctorate to become a microbiology researcher, she told them she knew what she wanted and she was going to get it.

People told me I'd never make it in hockey. Especially after I got cut from my high school team. But their doubts were fuel to my fire. I refused to be outworked.

I'd be so damn proud to have Lainey on my arm. She's a strong, smart, beautiful woman who doesn't let anyone put her in a box. It might not be fair for me to shoot my shot with her when she's ready, but I don't think I could forgive myself if I didn't at least try.

———

"No way!" Lainey laughs as she scrolls through the photos on Suki's phone from yesterday. "How long did it take to clean him up?"

"Hours," Carter grumbles. "It wasn't just him. There was mud all over the house. Wait 'til you get to the one of the shower."

Mara is sitting next to Lainey, and she howls with laughter when she sees one of the pictures. Suki told us she and the girls were walking Darling yesterday and he bolted for the muddy front yard of a house under construction. By the time they got home, Darling, Suki and all the girls were covered in mud.

A few months ago, Carter had a contractor build onto their garage. They added a big bathroom with an oversized walk-in shower for Darling because he got too big to fit in their regular tubs and showers.

"Aw." Lainey meets Suki's gaze. "The one of Darling putting his snout right up in Carter's face."

"That's my favorite," Hallie says.

I snicker because I was the first one Suki passed the phone to, and I saw how pissed Carter was as he scrubbed their pet pig. He even had to wash mud off his ass.

"No more walks," Carter says. "He gets plenty of exercise in the yard."

"I agree," Suki says.

We finished dinner, which turned out amazing. Harry raved about Lainey's bread, which actually was the best bread I've ever tasted. Now we're all sitting around my dining room table, which is being used for the first time ever, talking over after-dinner drinks.

"Olivia, how are the figure skating lessons going?" I ask.

"Good. It's fun."

"She's doing great," Carter says.

They set her up with private lessons with Sam Granger, a former Olympic figure skater who lives in Cleveland. Charlotte plays hockey and Hallie takes all kinds of different lessons but loves gymnastics most.

"You guys did so much work on that amazing dinner. Let us clean up the kitchen," Suki says.

"No, we're not worrying about any of that until later," Lainey says.

She and Suki keep talking, but I don't really hear what they're saying. I'm completely hung up on how Lainey looks tonight. She's wearing a little black thing she called a romper.

It's low cut, a one-piece outfit with wide, short sleeves and shorts. Her hair is loose around her shoulders and when I was close to her in the kitchen earlier, I smelled perfume on her that I swear is laced with sex pheromones.

I don't think I've ever seen her laugh and smile as much as she has tonight. Harry brought her a bottle of wine and a candle and I caught myself feeling a flare of jealousy when she hugged him.

There's no reason to be jealous—Harry's gay and has recently been on a couple of dates with a landscape architect who apparently has *delicious biceps.* I'm just so sex-starved that I'm low-key jealous of anything Lainey strokes. She wrapped her hand around the neck of a bottle of wine earlier, and yeah...I started to get hard.

"Tomorrow's gonna hurt," Carter says to me.

I tear my gaze away from Lainey. "Huh?"

He smirks. "The workout tomorrow. After all that food."

"Oh. Yeah, probably."

No one's mentioned Shane all night. Could it really be this easy? Is Lainey already over him?

I don't want to be the guy she falls into bed with right after a breakup and regrets. But I don't know how long I can keep pretending I just want to be a friend to her.

How long is long enough to wait? A month? It hasn't even been a week. And hell, she might not even want me back.

Wouldn't that be ironic if, now that I've come around to finally see the incredible woman she is, she's over me?

I can't even think about that.

CHAPTER FOURTEEN

Lainey

A FEW HOURS LATER, I'm still smiling as I close the dishwasher door and push the button to start it.

"I really enjoyed today," I say, hanging the dish towel in my hand over the bar on the stove.

"So did I."

That deep, husky voice gets me every time. Bash would sound sexy saying literally anything. And now, I don't have to feel guilty for thinking so because I'm single.

I'm still not fully used to it. I never thought I'd be single again. It doesn't feel bad; it just feels different.

Bash is wiping down the counters and Bruce is curled up on the rug in front of the sink. It's the first time I've been at his house on the weekend. I explored Cleveland to avoid him the first weekend and I was at Mara's last weekend.

"Your range was everything I hoped it would be." I smooth a hand over the front of his sleek, high-end kitchen appliance. "I can't wait to make more sourdough in it."

He finishes wiping the counters and washes his hands, then takes off his backward baseball cap and runs a hand through his hair. "I'm glad you like it."

Awareness dances down my spine as he looks at me, his arms folded. I must be imagining there's an intensity in his gaze. Or maybe I'm mistaking the look of a concerned friend for something else.

"How are you feeling?" he asks.

"A little tired." I laugh lightly. "Believe it or not, making sourdough can be stressful."

He scoffs. "Fuck yeah, I believe it."

"I'm not usually that bad. But knowing Harry was going to eat it, I wanted it to be my best."

He comes closer to me until I'm standing with my back against the island counter and he's right across from me, his back to the kitchen counter.

"Has Shane contacted you?"

I shake my head. "I think he knows that door is closed."

"And how are you feeling about that?"

I consider. "Pretty good, actually. I've been thinking about what this means for me. I was planning to stay in Ohio, but now..." I smile. "Stanford has an incredible program for me to get my doctorate. There's also a place in Cambridge and one in Israel that are dream research jobs. I can go anywhere."

Bash's expression is serious. "Yeah, but...that's really far away."

"It doesn't matter, though. I'm spending this entire year on research, even though I don't know where I'll be next semester. I'm seriously considering applying to the Cambridge and Israel places. Why not?"

He takes a step forward, now standing so close I have to crane my neck to keep our eyes locked.

"Don't run away," he says gruffly. "I know you're hurt, but you won't be proving anything to anyone by running to the other side of the world."

I laugh lightly. "That's not it at all, though. I didn't think I could even consider those places and now I'm not tied down."

He puts a palm on the island right beside me and

then does the same with his other hand, so close now that I can feel the heat of his body. My heart races with anticipation.

"Maybe you need to consider other options."

My breathing turns shallow. What's happening here? I'm an empirical person—I like facts and verifiable data more than vibes. But everything in me is telling me that Bash is talking about *him*.

Facts: he's so close I can feel him and smell his addictive cologne; he's giving me sex eyes; he's looking dead serious as he tells me to consider things that don't involve me leaving the country.

"Wha..." I clear my throat. "What do you mean?"

His lips quirk slightly. He eases closer to me, sliding a foot between mine. I lean back, gasping as his chest meets mine.

"I know you're newly single, but I'm saying maybe you'll consider a real man who knows he's damn lucky to even have a chance with you."

He glances at my cleavage and then his eyes flick back up to mine, hunger swirling in them.

I realize all at once what he's doing, and my heart plummets to my feet. Bash assumes my confidence is in the gutter because of Shane. He wants me to know there are other men out there who will want me.

But this—letting me believe he could ever be one of those men—is messing with my head. That girl who adored him from afar will always be part of me. Maybe she's an even bigger part of me now that I see how much Bash cares for me as a friend.

Every time he does something sweet, like stock the pantry with Dr Pepper and frosted cherry Pop-Tarts, my stomach does a little flutter. It's like a cruel sneak peek at what life could have been like if he loved me back.

Cooking together. Long evenings laughing with friends. Quick goodbyes as I rush out the door in the morning, perennially running just on time. Add in great sex, and that's the dream.

"I don't know." I shift and he moves away from the island. "But it's okay either way, Bash. Really. I don't need men thinking I'm sexy to know I'm worthy. There's more to life than that."

He looks disappointed, like his effort to boost my confidence failed.

"I promise I'm good. I'm actually excited about having my options open. I just want to have fun and research the hell out of the human microbiome."

He smiles playfully. "Aren't those one and the same for you?"

"Absolutely. I'm a massive gut enthusiast."

His smile slides away. "All I'm saying is, keep an open mind. Don't overlook what's standing right in front of you."

Is he...? Damn, why can't I be as good at reading social cues as I am at reading technical research papers? I'm not brave enough to ask if he means him because the first round of total and complete humiliation was enough.

"You've been such a great friend to me since I got here," I say softly. "Even when I didn't appreciate it."

"You're special to me, Lane."

My cheeks warm with embarrassment. "Was I the first one to profess my undying love?"

"The only." His lips quirk with amusement.

"Ha. That's not true. I've been on social media and seen all the women lusting after Sebastian Stone. There are hashtags about wanting to get boned by Stone."

His smile is sheepish. "Yeah, but that's just women who look at me and like what they see. They don't know me."

I use my hands to slide up and sit on the kitchen island, rolling my eyes. "It must be so hard for you, having women after you all the time."

"It doesn't mean anything. When you came to see me that day, to tell me how you felt about me—"

I bury my face in my hands. "God, no. I thought we had silently agreed to never talk about this."

"It meant a lot," he says softly. "Because you know me. But you know there was no way I could reciprocate, right? I was twenty-one and you were seventeen. I couldn't risk even the image of anything improper."

Despite my flaming cheeks, I move my hands away and look at him. "I'm willing to talk about this for like forty-five seconds, and that's it. You never need to apologize, Bash. I was a goofy teenager and I totally get it. You rejected me as nicely as you could have."

"But you know I *couldn't*, right?"

A knot forms in my stomach. Even after all this time, it's so uncomfortable to talk about this. I won't let him gloss over the truth, though, no matter how much I want to talk about literally anything else.

"You didn't want me back," I say quietly. "It wasn't that you wanted me back and *couldn't* do anything."

He exhales heavily. "That's true. But it's because, at twenty-one, I never would have even let myself want a seventeen-year-old."

He's still trying to convince me I'm not a loser no

man will ever want. I don't know why he thinks I need this pep talk.

"Okay, listen," I say. "I know who I am. I'm not for everyone. I snort when I laugh hard and I'm a science nerd. I usually spend less than a minute a day on my hair. I love reading and watching TV way more than going out. I'm a good listener. I make a damn good sourdough. I like taking care of people. If I find a man someday who sees all of this—" I gesture in a circle at myself, "And he happens to be quirky and cute and amazing too, and we get each other, maybe I'll be in a relationship again. I know what I deserve. It's a lot more than what Shane was giving me. You don't need to build me up or reassure me. I promise I'm good."

He nods. "I know you are."

I slide down from the island. "I'm going to bed. It's going to be a long week in the lab, so don't worry about me. I'm helping the professor teach a unit on the research I'm doing, so I'll have to do lab stuff in the evenings. I'll be home late every night, and I'll eat before I get here."

"I'm starting training camp, so I won't be around much, either."

"Who are we leaving in charge? Bruce or Dough Goldberg?"

He grins. "River will be here soon. He'll be in charge-ish."

I furrow my brow. "What does that mean?"

"You'll see. He tried to teach Bruce yoga last year and Bruce took a shit on the yoga mat."

Bruce thumps his tail on the rug when he hears his name. Or because he's proud of shitting on the yoga mat.

"So I guess I'll see you when I see you," I say.

"Yeah. Don't let those college guys get hot for teacher."

"Me?" I laugh. "Did you ever get hot for any of your teachers?"

"No comment."

"Well, you always did like older women."

He looks me up and down. "When I was a teenager, yeah. But I'm twenty-eight now. Younger women can be sexy as fuck."

My heart practically trembles at the thought of him finding *me* sexy. But that's not what he's saying...is it?

I head upstairs, turning to call over my shoulder. "You don't need to reassure me, Bash. I know someone will be attracted to me again someday."

"Maybe someone already is."

Since my back is facing him, I can safely grin so

big that my cheeks ache. Whether he's trying to build my confidence or he's actually flirting with me, his words are making me warm all over.

And I really like it.

CHAPTER FIFTEEN

Three Weeks Later
Bash

"AND NOW IT'S time for a Cleveland Crush POWER PLAY!"

The announcer's voice booms throughout the arena, the crowd roaring. We're playing a preseason game against Atlanta, so the stands aren't full, but there's a decent crowd.

Leo charges down the ice, our line's power forward making me and Carter look slow. I'm a solid skater, so I get myself where I need to be as quickly and efficiently as I can.

Carter passes me the puck. I immediately find

Leo and pass it to him. We practiced this play a lot in camp. No one expects Leo to even shoot the puck, so...

"That's a Crush goal!" the announcer says after Leo slapshots the puck into the net.

We form a circle on the ice to celebrate scoring, the defensemen joining us.

"Let's get another one!" Carter says.

The preseason is slower than the regular season, but it doesn't last long, and it's got me back in my routine again. No more sitting around fantasizing about Lainey while she's at the lab.

Now I fantasize about her while I'm at our practice facilities. We haven't seen much of each other in the past three weeks. If we do, it's usually on the weekend, and it's not for long.

Suki and the girls came over last weekend to bake with Lainey. She showed them how to use sourdough to make cinnamon rolls, and the girls gave Suki and Lainey makeovers.

Even with blue eyeshadow and bright-red lipstick, Lainey is still sexy. It actually got me going to imagine smearing that lipstick and asking her if she looked slutty just for me.

I'm a bad man. A dirty one. I could never tell Lainey about all the filthy things I want to do and say to her. Even if I pursue her, it'll be in a gentle-manly way. I can never tell my best friend's sister I want her to be my whore. I love dirty talk, but I don't think she would.

Which is okay. I can just think about the things I want to say.

I had hoped that seeing less of her would help. Make my attraction less of a growing physical need to be near her. But it had the opposite effect. I wait for her in the kitchen every morning just so I can see her sweep past me with a quick goodbye as she rushes out the door.

After a line change, I catch my breath on the bench, squirting water into my mouth from my water bottle. It feels good to be back. To have more places to put my energy.

"Sutton's sluggish as hell," Carter says from next to me.

"Yeah, he's heavier."

Preseason games are where rosters get shored up and lines get finalized. Morris Sutton, who plays for Atlanta, faces the double whammy of being thirty-six and slacking on conditioning in the offseason. He used to be great, but now he's a guy who's hanging on too long.

"Don't let me become him," I tell Carter.

He scoffs. "Are you kidding? I'll tell you you're out of shape all day, every day. And when it's time for you to go, I'll shove your ass out the door if I have to. You guys will do the same for me."

"Yeah."

One of our third-line forwards, Jack Randolph, meets my gaze as he skates toward the bench. It's a signal telling me to take over for him. I climb over the wall and dig in, diving to intercept the puck when it flies my way. Randolph is trying to come back after knee surgery, and so far, the preseason's been tough for him.

Isaac, our goalie, loses his edge in the third period, causing us to drop the game. A final score of 5–2 is shitty when you're the team with the two, even in the preseason.

Coach Turner looks somber when he comes into the locker room.

"Doubles starting tomorrow."

That's all he says. We all sit like statues, not making a sound as he leaves the locker room for his office. A single groan could turn double practices into something even worse.

Turner is the embodiment of fuck around and find out. Most coaches at the highest level of the game don't bag skate their guys, which is a grueling punishment that involves skating long and hard enough that people are puking. Turner bag skates us when he thinks we deserve it.

It sucks, but I think he's right to do it. A complacent coach has complacent players. Complacent teams don't win championships.

Leo comes over to me and Carter, one towel around his neck and another wrapped around his waist.

"That was ugly," he says.

"Yeah, no shit." Carter runs a hand over his face.

"We should come in early tomorrow and drill," I say.

"Yeah. Good idea." Carter nods and looks between the two of us. "Six thirty?"

"Yep." I check the time on my phone.

Shit. It's after ten thirty p.m. I need to get home and go to bed. Practice starts at eight tomorrow, and instead of going until noon, it'll go until four. Then there's a team dinner Carter and Suki are hosting. And then there's the thing after that, which I'm going to need a few drinks in me to be able to do.

I'll have to be up at five thirty tomorrow to be on the ice at six thirty. But that's what a good first line does; we set the tone for our entire team. Almost all of us looked like minor leaguers in that game, and Atlanta's not even a top team.

The team provides breakfast and lunch on weekdays, so at least I know I can get some protein before practice officially starts tomorrow.

I won't even be able to see Lainey in passing tomorrow. But she's meeting me at the team dinner.

She's going home to Columbus this weekend because her niece, Avana, is turning three. I hate that I have to miss it, but I'll be traveling with the team. Though I've tried to make it obvious I'm interested in her, she doesn't seem to be getting it.

I was driving to the practice facility a couple of days ago when it finally hit me. She went out on a limb for me. She risked hurt and rejection. I have to do the same. But I'm going to do it on an even bigger scale. And I'm doing it before she goes to Columbus this weekend because she could see Shitty Shane.

It's not likely, but just in case. It's been almost a month since they broke up. I'm not taking any chances, though. I'm ready to shoot my shot.

Hopefully it won't be an air ball, because I'm going to have an audience.

CHAPTER SIXTEEN

Lainey

THE SMOKY, caramelized scent of grilled meat greets me when I walk into Harvest Moon. I'm not letting myself eat it because of my IBS, but I can at least enjoy the smell.

The chicken will be delicious, too. Harry and his team don't know how to cook anything that's not delicious.

I went to a downtown Cleveland boutique on my lunch and splurged on an emerald-green strapless dress. It hits just above my knees. I'm wearing a simple black shrug and black sandals with it. It might be the dressiest outfit I own.

Suki told me the women get pretty dressy at this team dinner, and when I see a woman walk by me in a flowy gown, I'm really glad she prepared me.

"Damn." Bash approaches me, his arms open and his grin wide. "You look incredible, Lane. You're sexy as hell in that dress."

My stomach flutters as he embraces me. I haven't seen him much lately. Tonight, he's wearing a light-gray suit with a dark-blue dress shirt beneath, the top button of his shirt undone. His wavy dark hair has been tamed into a combed-back style, a stubborn lock of hair falling over his forehead.

He just said I'm *sexy*. And he smells so good. Also, his muscles. My brain is short-circuiting from sensory overload.

"How was your day?" he murmurs.

"Pretty good."

His deep laugh sends his warm breath brushing over my ear. "Did I just feel your stomach growling?"

I pull back, grinning sheepishly. "I didn't have time for lunch."

"C'mon."

He takes my hand and leads me toward a side room of the restaurant. Carter and Suki rented out the entire place for this dinner. They invited every player, coach, staffer and their families. I'm a little bit early and there are already more than fifty people here.

There's a long row of tables set up along one wall of the side room, and it's filled with appetizers. Bash releases my hand and grabs a plate. I follow his lead.

"Hey, Lainey," Leo says from nearby. "You haven't been able to get rid of this asshole yet?"

Bash flips him off. I'm too busy loading up my little plate with as much food as I can fit on it. Shrimp cocktail, caprese skewers and stuffed mushrooms. Yes, yes, and hell yes. I'm not risking the bacon-wrapped jalapeño poppers Bash took four of, but they look amazing.

"How's your day going?" I ask as I join Bash at a little standing table.

"Ugh. Better now. I spent seven hours on the ice today."

"Wow, why?"

"Double practices, plus some extra drills. Which we need, but it still takes a lot out of us."

"You can eat double dessert tonight with no guilt, though."

He barks a single note of laughter. "If I want to feel like I ate an elephant tomorrow at five thirty a.m. when I wake up to do it all over again."

"Aw, poor Bash," I tease. "All work and no play."

He's about to respond when Hallie and Charlotte approach us. Charlotte is wearing a simple, pretty blue dress with a simple white headband in her short pink pixie cut. Hallie's dress is purple with a full skirt, her curls loose.

"Look at you two," I say, stepping back from our table to admire them. "Beautiful!"

Hallie does a little curtsy. Charlotte gives me a half smile and I sense that she didn't choose her outfit herself.

"We snuck out of the kids' room to ask you how many stars there are in the sky," Hallie says.

"The kids' room?"

Charlotte shrugs. "Dex and Mara are helping us do a craft. Mara said *motherfucker* when she cut her finger on a staple gun."

I arch my brows, amused. "And you left that to come here?"

"It's a million, isn't it?" Hallie blurts. "I told her it's a million, but she doesn't believe me."

"I think it's infinity," Charlotte explains. "No one's ever counted all of them because there are so many."

"Those are both excellent guesses."

"Yeah, but who's right?" Hallie presses.

"Well, you know how we can look up at the sky

at night and see stars? In the entire sky, if it's completely clear, there are around nine thousand visible stars."

"That's close to a million," Hallie says.

"No, it's not!" Charlotte gapes at her.

I exchange a smile with Bash.

"You know how we live in a galaxy?" I say.

Both girls nod.

"Well, scientists estimate there are about two trillion galaxies in our universe. That's a number so big we can't really even comprehend it. And in every one of those galaxies, there are billions to trillions of stars. We don't have a total number, but it would be very, very large if we did."

"I want to be a star scientist," Hallie says.

"An astronomer? You should."

"An astromoner."

"It's *astronomer*, Hals," Charlotte says.

Mara comes into the room, a white bandage wrapped around one of her index fingers.

"Girls, what are you doing in here? You're supposed to be working on your posters." She smiles at me and puts an arm around my shoulders. "Hey. I'm helping the kids make posters for the locker room."

"Do you guys get to eat?"

"Yeah, Harry fed us before everyone else got here. I'm sure I'll also have some of the mac and cheese they're making for the kids." She looks from Bash to me. "I hear we're going out after this."

I pinch my brows together in surprise. "We are?"

"Mara, why don't you take the girls back to the other room?" Bash says, looking aggravated.

"Oh. Was I not supposed to say anything?"

My cheeks warm as Mara puts an arm around each of the girls and walks away.

"It's completely okay if it's a team thing and I'm not invited," I say. "I'm wiped out and I want to go right home after this, anyway."

He shakes his head. "No, you have to come."

"We'll see. Maybe for one drink."

"That's not gonna work, Lane."

I laugh. "Oh really?"

"You'll see why. We're going out after this, and you'll have a blast."

"Even though I'm a tired introvert?"

"It'll be fun. I promise."

———

OKAY, so it's fun. A bunch of players and their plus ones are at The Factory for karaoke night.

It's crowded, and so far, we've been treated slash subjected to "I Will Always Love You" by Whitney Houston, "Every Rose Has Its Thorn" by Poison and "Sweet Caroline" by Neil Diamond.

Bash has his arm around my shoulders, and I don't mind at all. He had his arm around my waist when we joined the entire bar in belting out "Sweet Caroline."

I don't think it's the alcohol. He had two beers and one shot at dinner and he's been nursing the same beer since we got here.

"You having a good time?" he asks me.

"I am. You were right."

"You should sing a song with the girls."

I laugh. "Yeah, I don't think so."

"Aw, come on. Bet you'd like it. Have you ever sung at a karaoke bar?"

"Me? No. Are you serious? Have you?"

"Nope."

"Okay, guys," the DJ says. "Up next, we have Bash and the Boyz. Spelled with a Z, which means this is either going to be really good or really bad."

Bash removes his arm from around my shoulders. "That's my cue."

"What? You're singing?"

He takes a long swig from his beer bottle. "Wish me luck."

My jaw drops. "Okay...good luck? What are you singing?"

He winks at me. "You'll see."

Several of his teammates follow him onto the stage. I glance at Suki, who is grinning, her chin resting on her steepled hands as she looks at the stage. Harry and Mara both have their phone cameras ready to record.

Why does it feel like everyone except me knows what's going on? I try to look like I'm in on the joke as Bash takes the mic from the DJ. Carter, Leo, Silas and Isaac gather behind him, all of them loose and happy from the shots they've been doing.

The opening notes to "Take On Me" by A-ha start playing. He's singing an '80s classic! I laugh, feeling giddy. Good thing Harry and Mara are immortalizing this in video—this song has some high notes.

He starts singing, and it's possibly the funniest cover of a song I've ever heard. Bash's voice is way too deep for this one, and he's not a singer. But his eyes are locked onto me and he's smiling confidently. I clap and cup my hands around my mouth, cheering for him.

Then he gets to the chorus. Instead of singing the

words *take on me*, he sings, *come to prom*. My smile drops away. What is this?

His teammates are swaying back and forth with their arms around each other. Singing their part of the song with him right after his lyric, which is *go to prom with him*.

"Get it, Bash!" Dex yells, clapping.

Every time he sings the chorus, he sings it the same way, *come to prom*. His teammates join him, all of them in a group, as Bash unabashedly belts out the highest notes of the song.

The entire bar is cheering for him. I'm laughing, but I also have tears in my eyes. There's a massive knot in my stomach. Bash wouldn't make fun of me. He wouldn't. But still, I'm wondering if this song is him making fun of me asking him to prom.

Near the end of the song, he walks down from the stage and comes over to me. The whole bar is hooting and hollering as he gets onto his knees.

"Lane, I don't just want to be your friend," he says, his expression turning serious.

My heart hits the floor and I can't help it—the tears roll down my cheeks.

"I want so much more," he continues. "And I want to start by doing what I couldn't do seven years ago. Will you go to prom with me?"

My jaw drops. I swipe my fingertips over my cheeks to clear them. Even though I don't know what's happening, I know this is the most shocking, absurd, amazing moment I've ever imagined.

"Prom?" I manage.

"Yeah. I'm having a prom just for you. And me. For us. All you have to do is say yes."

He takes my hand in his, hope swirling in his eyes. I can't believe this is real. It's everything my younger self dreamed of. Actually, it's more because Bash did this himself. I didn't imagine it.

He wanted to. And he did.

"Yes." I squeeze his hand. "I'll go to prom with you."

Everyone around us is yelling and cheering. Bash hands off the microphone and embraces me, my feet leaving the ground as he lifts me up so we're eye to eye.

His lips are on mine. My heart backflips wildly as he kisses me. The kiss is soft and sweet, but there's certainty, too. Like he's been waiting forever for it and there's no doubt in his mind.

I'm breathless and a little dizzy when he sets me back down, everyone around us still cheering.

"We're going to prom?"

It's September—not the right time of year to

crash a high school prom. But Bash just rewrote the chorus to a classic '80s song to invite me to one, so I can't help wondering what's in store.

He gives me that sexy grin I never really got over. "You bet your ass we are."

He cups my cheek and kisses me again. I still feel like I'm in an alternate reality.

It's happening, though. And if I have further doubts, there's video evidence.

I'm almost twenty-five years old, and I'm going to my first prom.

CHAPTER SEVENTEEN

Bash

I TAP Leo's shoulder as we wait to climb the stairs to board our team plane. He turns and pulls one of his AirPods out.

"Did you know "Just a Friend" by Biz Markie is actually an '80s song? Came out in '89."

"Fascinating," he deadpans.

"It's got a '90s vibe."

"I guess."

He turns around, but I catch him before he puts his Air Pod back in. "Should I put it on the prom playlist or not?"

He scrunches his brow and gives me a look. "You gonna dance to that song?"

"I mean...I could."

"Please don't."

The line to get on the plane moves and I climb the stairs, putting my phone in my pocket. It's six a.m. and we're boarding our first flight to an away game for the season.

Preseason, actually. The routine is the same, though. We're all a little hungover from the team dinner last night, so it's quiet this morning.

Our new defender, Anson Hunt, is sitting in my usual seat. I stop in the aisle and shift, then sigh deeply.

"What?" he asks.

"I usually sit there."

"I'm not moving."

I pretend not to care. It's killing my vibe, though. I've been on a high since last night when I made a fool of myself in front of hundreds of people and it paid off.

But on game days, my routine is everything. I get on the plane, I sit in the same seat every time, and I eat ten cashews and drink half a bottle of water before we take off.

Always the same seat. Always ten cashews. Salted.

If they were unsalted, that would ruin my vibe, too. I'm not neurotic about much, but I'm super fucking neurotic about my game-day routine.

"Whatever, guess we'll just lose," I mutter as I keep walking.

Another part of my routine is my playlists. Once I'm sitting in the wrong seat, I count out my cashews and start eating them while I pull up my travel playlist.

"That's What I Like" by Bruno Mars starts playing. I lean back and close my eyes, eating my first cashew while I start my visualizing process.

Our team owner, Hudson McClain, has a sports psychologist work with us on mindset from time to time. You could be in top shape physically, but if your head's not in the right place, you're fucked.

After dropping our first preseason game, we're all in a mood. I can shake off losses when I'm not with my teammates, but practices and travel are different when we're not winning. They're quieter. Partially because Coach works us until we're all about to collapse at practice.

He took it easier on us yesterday afternoon because he wanted us to be ready to play today. We did light drills and yoga. I'm pretty sure he wasn't thrilled about any of us drinking alcohol at the team dinner last night. Or that we went out afterward.

Too fucking bad. I needed to put myself out there for Lainey, just like she did for me. She did it at just seventeen years old, which is badass. I wanted to up the stakes, so I put my feelings out there in public, with my teammates watching.

I was prepared for her to be confused. Adults don't usually invite each other to prom. But I hoped she'd see my sincerity and trust that I knew what I was doing.

When we got home last night, she told me she was completely exhausted and needed to go to bed, but she asked me if I was serious about the prom thing. I told her I was completely serious and it was in nine days.

I wanted to kiss her again. Wanted a hell of a lot more than that, actually. But I'm waiting until after our first date. So I kissed the back of her hand and went to bed with a hard-on, as usual.

I finish my cashews, then imagine myself skating onto the ice tonight. I'm tougher than those Denver fucks. I want this win more. My focus is entirely on the puck. Its position and my position. Scoring tonight is everything. I picture myself slapshotting the puck into the net. Sliding it around from the back. Edging it in. Making an open net shot. Scoring in a shoot-off.

The sports psychologist taught us a mental exercise. It's new age and kind of fucked up, but I like the frame of mind it puts me in, so I do it.

I score goals all the time. I find openings where others can't. Nothing affects my mindset during a game. All I care about when the clock is running is putting the puck in the net.

I envision celebrating with my team tonight in Denver's brand-new arena. Our sticks are up and everyone's smiling. It's a blowout. We're winners.

Though I'd prefer to be thinking about Lainey, I can't today. My mind has to be entirely on the game. I get paid a lot to perform at the highest level. All that offseason training won't mean shit if I let myself slip mentally.

My seat's beside a window, so I use a blanket as a pillow and zone out, hoping to sleep.

Tomorrow, I can let my mind wander wherever it wants. Today is about winning.

———

MY TEAMMATES like to stand in a circle and kick a

soccer ball around during the afternoon lag between napping and getting dressed for a game.

But me, I like to spend this part of the day in a mental fortress. I'm keeping all my energy in reserve. With my headphones on and my pregame pump list playing, I walk.

It's a leisurely walk; I hardly even break a sweat. I have a course charted in every area, but I'm still familiarizing myself with the new Denver one. My walks are in the lowest-trafficked places I can find. I don't want to stop and talk, but sometimes I'm forced to when we're on the road.

At home, everyone who works at the arena knows I'm down to wave or nod, but I don't want to stop. This is part of my process.

I'm listening to "Enter Sandman" by Metallica. Walking helps keep me loose while conserving energy. The tunnel we'll all be in later is empty now, and I'm about to turn a corner when a ding in my headphones tells me I just got a text.

Eric: I just found out about you and Lainey when my receptionist showed me a video of you singing to her. WTF.

I stop, blowing out a breath.

Bash: I'm shooting my shot. I love you, but I don't care if you approve.

Eric: Fine. But if you hurt her, I'll hurt you. Clear?

Bash: Clear. You and Callie can come to the prom I'm having for Lainey if you want.

Eric: Sounds like a cheese fest...

Bash: Okay, granddad. Stay home and count your nose hairs.

Eric: Fuck you. Send me the details and I'll check with Cal.

Bash: I will. gtg it's game day.

Eric: Try this time, ok? That last game was a joke.

Bash: yep

I quickly type out the date, location and time of the prom, then resume walking. Eric's comment about the last game is in my head now. That means I have to return to visualizing. This is why I don't like any distractions on game days.

It's hard to get my head into the right place for a game. It takes time, concentration, and effort to minimize distractions. And it can all be undone in a matter of seconds.

Not that he's wrong. But that game is in the past, and I'm focused on today.

Any player who doesn't get how much of this game is mental isn't going to make it. The physical stuff is somewhat out of our control, like with aging and injuries. But the mental part is what you really have to master if you want to play this game long term.

I have to do my part tonight—for my line and for my team.

———

"LET ME SEE," our team trainer Melina says with an edge. "Stop moving."

"Just glue it shut so I can get back out there."

I took a high stick hit to my face and I'm bleeding. But it's the third period and when Melina dragged me back to the locker room, we were only up by one goal. It's 3–2, and I've scored two of our goals. I want a hat trick, even though it's only the preseason.

Melina pours water on my brow, dabs at the cut with gauze, and hisses through her teeth. "Yeah, that's deep. You want to stitch it now?"

We just got a new team doctor. Her name's Caroline and she's too slow and cautious for my liking.

"Just glue it and get me back out there!" I bark before Caroline can answer.

"Easy, cowboy." That's Caroline. "I have to stitch this one."

I groan, frustrated. "Can you not spend an hour

talking about it? I don't need anesthetic. Just get it done."

I'm lying on an exam table, and she looks down at me, her smile unbothered. "You're done with this game, Sebastian. I have to trim your eyebrow before I can stitch."

"What the fuck?"

"We can't have hair in the wound."

"Great," I bark. "How short? Will it be obvious?"

"Yes. This is a deep laceration. And I can't let the hair I cut get into the wound, either. I might need to shave it."

Melina slides her lips into her teeth, fighting a smile.

I scowl. "Yeah, funny shit."

"We can draw one for you with a pencil." She busts out laughing. "Or dye your other one white so it blends in."

God. Damn. I'm going to look great for my first date with Lainey. One fucking eyebrow.

"Do you have clippers?" Caroline asks Melina.

"Yeah, let me find some." Melina checks her phone. "Carter just scored! We're up 4–2!"

I relax a little. We're so close to the end of the game that a two-goal lead should be enough for the win. That's what really matters. I'd rather have one eyebrow and a win than a loss.

"You ready?" Caroline asks me a few minutes later.

My eyebrow is gone and my teammates are back in the locker room celebrating the win. I'm in a side room, and Carter and Leo come in together.

"You okay, man?" Carter asks.

"Yeah, the doc's about to stitch me up."

"Are we waiting until she's done to comment on the eyebrow?" Leo asks.

I sigh heavily. "I don't give a fuck."

"At least it wasn't a tooth," Carter says. "Eyebrows grow back."

"You'll still be able to give half-dirty looks," Leo quips.

"Okay, here comes the numbing shot," Caroline says.

"I told you I don't need it."

"You do, though. This cut is deep. The good news is your eyebrow will cover most of the scar—when it grows back."

Carter puts a hand on my shoulder. "Relax, man. I'll tell Suki to let Lainey know you're gonna live."

Lainey. I didn't even think about her watching this game and seeing me taken away bleeding. She said she was planning to watch the game with Bruce tonight.

"Yeah, thanks," I say.

"Can you feel this?" Caroline asks.

"Nope."

"Okay then. Close your eyes and keep your face completely relaxed. If you feel any pain or pulling, let me know."

"Okay." I close my eyes, then open them again. "This won't keep me out for the next game, will it?"

"It shouldn't. As long as the swelling goes down, and it should with ice and an anti-inflammatory, and this cut stays clean, you'll be fine to play the next game."

I close my eyes, better now that I know that. Nothing's keeping me from the opening game of the season with my team. I could have one eye and I'd be out there with an eye patch.

We all worked hard in the offseason, and we're ready to give our fans the season of a lifetime.

CHAPTER EIGHTEEN

Lainey

"Dang. My boobs look amazing in this dress."

I turn slightly in front of Mara's full-length bedroom mirror, admiring the fit of the fitted, floor-length sapphire gown I'm wearing. There are sparkly little crystals sewn into the bodice, trailing away past my waistline. The strapless cut emphasizes my full breasts, as does the hundred-and-ten-dollar bra I bought. I didn't own a strapless one, and this one pushes my breasts up perfectly.

"You just have amazing boobs," Mara says. "That dress is lucky to be touching them, and Bash will be, too."

I laugh, giving myself one more appreciative look before I turn to face her and Suki. "This must be what a wedding day is like. Where everyone knows you're having sex that night."

"Not my wedding day," Suki quips.

"Really?"

"Long story, but we hardly knew each other. I fell for my husband after we were already married."

"I want to hear that story at some point if you're okay sharing it."

"Of course."

Suki looks like a goddess in a red halter-cut gown that hugs her curves just right. Her long hair is styled in big waves and she's waiting for Mara to do her makeup. We decided to go full high school and get ready together at Mara's apartment.

Mara is wearing a short, black-sequined dress. Her dark hair, which she usually wears flowing down her back, is straightened and styled in a French knot at her neckline. She's a walking thirst trap, and I don't know how she's still single.

I didn't know what to do with my hair, so I let Mara decide. She put loose curls in it and then did a half-down, half-up style I love, with loose pieces framing my face. I don't think I've ever looked so elegant.

Mara has a two-bedroom apartment, and she has a lighted vanity for hair and makeup in one room. She works on her own makeup while Suki and I slow dance.

"I'd dip you, but I'm not very coordinated," I say.

"I'm saving all my fanciness for tonight. Carter and I have been practicing the *Dirty Dancing* lift."

Mara gasps, meeting Suki's gaze in the mirror. "You whore! You already married a pro athlete and got three beautiful girls with zero vaginal stretching, and now you're doing the *Dirty Dancing* lift?"

"Nobody puts Suki in a corner." She grins and twirls me beneath her arm.

"At least I can dance with Dex," Mara murmurs. "Harry's going to be all wrapped up in his boyfriend all night."

"I can't wait to meet him," I say.

"Same." Suki does a sexy pose in front of the mirror. "You guys, I'm wearing crotchless undies for the first time. I sent my husband a photo of the bra and panties lying on the bed before I got dressed and he responded with a GIF of a cartoon dog with its tongue rolling across the floor."

Mara groans. "Just keep rubbing the salt in. You guys are both getting railed tonight and I'll be alone with my overworked vibe."

I laugh. "You're gorgeous. If you're not getting any, that's a choice."

"Right?" Suki says. "Carter has single teammates."

"Ugh. Who, Leo? Hard pass."

She finishes her makeup, then does mine and Suki's. We take a selfie of the three of us and I send it to my mom. Then we relax over a glass of wine until there's a knock on Mara's door.

My heart pounds as we all stand up.

"It's for you," Suki says.

She and Mara go into Mara's bedroom, leaving me to answer the door. When I do, Bash is standing there in a perfectly fitted tux. He's clean-shaven and his hair is tamed. This Bash is so much...broader and filled out than the high school guy I crushed on. He's all man, the affection and desire in his eyes directed at me.

"You look incredible." He slowly rakes his gaze down my body and back up again.

"Thanks." I take a deep breath, trying to calm my racing heart. "So do you. Come in."

He steps inside, a boxed corsage in hand. "Why are you already blushing? We haven't gotten to that part of the evening yet."

I go up in flames. I've never been so excited—or

so nervous. I've only eaten Club crackers today because I'm so worried about my IBS. Food is usually the cause of my flares, but stress can be, too.

This isn't stressful, really, but my nerves are pretty raw. I've been dreaming about Bash seeing me as more than a friend for so long. Even after he turned me down, my feelings never disappeared. I just learned to ignore them.

"Anything blush-inducing isn't guaranteed." My tone is a thousand times lighter than my stomach right now. "We'll have to see how things go."

He grins. "Understood. I was talking about making you blush with a goodnight kiss later. What were you thinking about?"

I suppress a smile. "Wouldn't you like to know?"

He closes the distance between us, snaking an arm around my waist and pulling me close. I inhale sharply, my palm flying to rest on his chest.

Damn. His body is just unfair. How can I speak full sentences when such a tall, broad, powerful man's body is flush with mine?

"Yes, please." His deep, eager tone makes me clench my thighs together. "I'd really fucking like to know."

"Jesus, Bash, are you going to start humping her

leg?" Mara's approaching voice makes Bash take a step back. "Corsage her and let's get this show on the road."

He flicks a glare in her direction and opens the corsage box. I didn't want anything I had to pin to my dress, and Suki must have told him. He got me an old-school wrist corsage, which is made of beautiful flowers in several shades of blue and accented with small white flowers.

Suki takes pictures as he puts it on me, and then she takes more of me pinning on his small corsage. It's completely unnecessary and silly, but it makes me smile anyway.

"Where's my date?" Suki asks.

"Waiting out front."

Bash has hired a limo for the evening, and when we walk out the front door of Mara's building, Carter is standing there smiling at Suki. We give them a minute of privacy by getting in the car, where Dex, Harry and Harry's boyfriend Aden are waiting.

"Damn, girl," Dex says to Mara when he sees her. "If I was straight, I'd take you home with me right now."

Aden and Harry are holding hands. Aden is handsome, his blond hair cut short. He has a short, well-groomed beard. Harry's giving him an adoring look. I force myself to play it cool, but they are ridiculously cute together.

"Aden, great to meet you," Bash says, shaking his hand. "I'm really glad you guys could make it tonight."

"Are you kidding?" Harry says. "I wasn't out yet in high school. I never thought I'd get to do this."

Carter has lipstick smeared on his lower lip when he climbs into the car. Suki wipes it away.

"Your eye looks better," Carter tells Bash.

"Yeah."

Suki convinced him to try on a fake eyebrow, which she trimmed out of a fake mustache, but apparently it looked so awful she laughed for five full minutes, so he's sporting his natural look tonight. It doesn't bother me in the least. I'm just glad his eye wasn't injured.

The limo drives us to a downtown warehouse that's been converted into an event venue. My stomach churns nervously as I try not to think about all the things I could do to embarrass myself.

Trip and fall—because heels. And I'd be one of those who stepped on my own dress and ripped it at the waist, exposing my ass to the world.

Spill something on my dress. Drop food into my cleavage. Break my water glass.

I want to be beautiful and polished for Bash. One false move, and he could remember I'm just Brainy Lainey in a fancy dress.

Bash takes my hand and leads me into the venue, my heart racing so fast I'm a little lightheaded.

As soon as we walk through the doors, I lose it. He rented out a massive space, big enough for a large wedding reception. There's a large table for dinner set on one end, and the rest is a huge dance floor.

It's decorated with purple floral arrangements and balloons, which is my favorite color. Twinkle lights sparkle on every post and are draped from the ceiling.

I didn't know he was going to do this much—just for me. I wipe tears from the corners of my eyes and look at him.

"I can't believe this. It's beautiful."

"I'm glad you like it. We're going to get pictures done before dinner."

My brows fly up. "Pictures?"

He spins me around, and I see photo props set up in one corner. There's a dark-purple backdrop, a white half pillar, and a purple and white balloon arch.

"How did you have time to do all this?" I ask, shaking my head with wonder.

"I hired someone. But the ideas were mine."

Dex and Mara are already posing for the photographer, her standing behind him with both arms wrapped around his midsection. I laugh, then lean up to kiss Bash's cheek.

"This is the nicest thing anyone's ever done for me."

His expression turns serious. "I'm all in. I want a chance to show you how much you mean to me."

There's a twist of something in my gut. I know I mean a lot to him. But if I fall completely in love with him, will I be the only woman he ever wants, forever?

"Are you sure you feel enough...attraction toward me?" I ask softly. "It's not just that you feel sorry for me?"

He narrows his eyes slightly. "I'm a thousand percent sure. I wanted to give you some time after the breakup, but yeah, I want you. So much I can hardly breathe."

I swallow hard, warmth rushing from my cheeks down. All I can do is nod.

Shane never made me feel this way. No one has. I didn't even realize it was possible for two people to be on fire for each other at the same time. At least not if one of those people is me.

But it's happening. Bash and I are seriously, for real, posing for prom photos. He's actually putting his hand on my ass as we get into the pose the photographer wants us in, and that's genuinely his erection I feel against my lower back.

Pinch me.

Maybe Bash will pinch me later. Preferably, my nipples. I can't believe I'm thinking that, but the idea of getting spanked and pinched by him is *hot*. I've always known I'm Velma on the streets and Daphne in the sheets. But no one else has.

Dinner is catered, Harry having nothing to do with it. Bash said he wanted Harry to enjoy tonight and not have anything to do with the menu.

There's salmon and chicken, risotto, and mixed vegetables. I only eat the chicken and veggies because there couldn't be a worse time for my IBS to show up.

My stomach has been churning since I laid eyes on Bash, though. I hope the food will settle my stomach.

We laugh like we've all been friends forever, Aden fitting in perfectly. When I spill a few drops of water on my chest, Bash winks, leans over and kisses that spot, making me hot all over. Even my arms are blushing—I don't even want to know what my face looks like.

"Dessert, are you serious?" Dex groans. "I'm so full already."

"Suck it up, you're gonna dance off every calorie," Mara says.

One of our servers is approaching with a rolling cart of silver dome-covered desserts, and she announces the selection as she pulls off the lids.

"Chocolate mousse with a gold leaf garnish, cheesecake with raspberry sauce and," She clears her throat. "Frosted cherry Pop-Tarts."

My chin drops. "What?"

Bash squeezes my hand beneath the table. "I know what my girl likes."

His girl. He just said that.

Everyone at the table politely ignores the tears in my eyes.

"I'm going to stuff that cheesecake into my mouth so hard," Mara says.

"You are one classy broad." Dex puts his cheek up against hers.

Of course I choose a Pop-Tart. And after we finish eating, a DJ comes out to start the music. He's a tall, fit Black man with a great smile.

"Hey, y'all, I'm DJ BJ and I'm ready to get this party started," he says, doing a raise-the-roof motion.

"DJ BJ," Dex says, a brow arched. "Sounds promising."

The first song is "Alone" by Heart, and Bash immediately pulls me close for a slow dance. He sings along so softly only I can hear him. My stomach is rolling, but I ignore it. I'm only open to happy vibes right now. Or horny, but that's under the happy umbrella.

It takes three songs for me to realize every song at this prom is from the '80s. Bash knows I love '80s songs. That man is so getting laid tonight, possibly even in the limo on the way home if we drop everyone else off first.

My feet ache from all the dancing by the time we all leave several hours later.

"This was the best evening I've ever had," I whisper in Bash's ear. "Thank you."

He gives me a soft, sweet kiss. "Same here."

The limo has just pulled away from the curb, heading for Harry's house, when a shot of pain hits me in the stomach.

No. This can't be happening. I've made it through this entire evening without tripping or nerding out about science. I have to make it back to Bash's.

The next cramp is like a bolt of lightning to my midsection. I cringe.

"You okay?" Bash asks, concerned.

Fucking irritable bowel syndrome. I did everything right tonight. I only drank water and ate chicken and noncruciferous vegetables. It has to be my nerves.

"I need a bathroom," I say, already mortified.

"Okay, we'll stop." He pushes a button to talk to the driver. "Hey, we need to stop at the nearest place with a bathroom, please."

"Yes, sir."

My cramps worsen. I clench my ass cheeks together, wishing I could tell Bash to just leave me here. He wouldn't, though.

It's happening. I'm going to shit. The only question is, will I make it to a bathroom in time?

"Sorry, guys," I mumble.

"Don't worry about it," Suki says. "There's a gas station in the next block, I'm sure he'll stop there."

"Nice," Mara says. "I can get a KitKat."

"I could go for some Takis," Aden says.

"Ooh, I love me some Takis," Mara says.

I'm clenching with everything I've got. Bash is

gently rubbing my neck, his hand beneath my hair. Tonight *can't* end with me shitting in the limo. It just cannot.

The limo slows and I intensify my clenching. I can't physically hold in the diarrhea, but if I have to, I will die trying.

We're turning. I see the glowing sign of a gas station. Bash pushes the button again.

"Take us right up to the front door," he says.

My desperation must be so obvious. If I don't make it, this will be the least of my humiliation.

As soon as the car stops, I open the door and fly out of it. I race to the front door and whip it open, picking up the skirt of my dress so I can run faster.

My sore feet are forgotten. There's only one thing I care about right now.

Must get to a toilet.

I see the *Restrooms* sign in a corner of the store. When I get there, I grab the handle to the women's room. I'm like three seconds away from losing control.

The door is locked. No!

I lunge at the door handle to the men's room. Unlocked. *Thank you, Jesus.*

Throwing the door open, I lock it with one hand

and pull my underwear down with the other. It's going to be a photo finish.

I pull the skirt of my dress up and wrap it around my waist, and I'm only two inches above the toilet seat when my body lets loose.

I made it. I almost cry with relief. I never thought I'd be so happy to be shitting in a dirty, smelly gas station bathroom.

CHAPTER NINETEEN

Bash

"I'M GOING to check on her," Mara says.

I shake my head. "Don't. She just has a sensitive stomach. She'll be fine."

She frowns. "Yeah, but shouldn't we at least ask her if she needs anything?"

Dex gives her a look. "She's not dying or anything."

Carter opens the limo's mini fridge. "You guys, Bash won't get charged for all of this unless we drink it. Who wants champagne?"

Suki raises an enthusiastic hand. "The girls are

with my parents for the weekend. I don't even need a glass. You can just pour it directly in my mouth."

He smirks. "Same thing you said this morning, babe. I'll fill your mouth up anytime you want."

Mara reaches for the mini fridge, covering her eyes with a hand. "Whatever I pull out, Dex and I will drink it all."

"I'm sorry, what?" he says.

She pulls out a small bottle of whiskey and everyone cheers. Everyone except Dex, who groans.

"I don't drink whiskey," he says.

"You do tonight!"

Mara opens the bottle and tips it to her lips, taking two swallows and then cringing hard. "Oh my God. It's like liquid fire."

She and Dex pass the bottle back and forth while everyone else tips their head back for Carter to pour champagne into their mouths. Even I drink some. Might as well since I'll get charged out the ass for it.

"Let's play a game," Harry says. "Have you ever had sex in a public place? Everyone has to answer."

"Yes," Mara says.

"No," Suki says.

"No," Carter says.

"Sadly, no," Dex says.

I consider. "Not really."

"I have," Harry says, looking sheepish.

Aden arches his brows. "Really? Mr. Adventurous over here. I haven't."

"Mara, what was the public place?" Dex asks.

"A grocery store."

Everyone gapes at her except Suki, who must have already known.

"You had sex at a grocery store?" Harry asks, incredulous.

"I was fucking a guy who stocked shelves at night. They were open twenty-four hours. He bent me over in the bread aisle."

Carter opens a tiny bottle of scotch from the minibar and downs it.

"That's fucking awful," he says, shaking his head. "Better have another one."

We continue our game, and it's my turn to come up with a question when Lainey opens the door to the limo and gets in.

"I'm so sorry, you guys," she says.

"Don't be," Suki says, waving a hand. "We're having a great time. It's Bash's turn to come up with the next Have You Ever question."

I put an arm around Lainey, exchanging a quick look with her to make sure she's okay. She gives me a small smile.

"Okay, it's not a *have you ever*, but what's your most embarrassing puking or shitting incident?"

Dex lifts up the bottle of whiskey in his hand. "I shit myself during a law school final."

"No!" Lainey says.

"I did. The professor told us we couldn't leave during the final or we'd fail the class. And it was property law, such a hard fucking class."

Mara groans. "The rule against perpetuities almost killed me."

"Wait, though." Carter scrunches his forehead. "Did he let you leave after you shit your pants?"

"He did." Dex shrugs. "I stayed in the bathroom until the class was over and my professor knocked on the door and told me I'd passed. I wasn't even halfway finished with it."

Carter laughs and takes another swig of the scotch as the car starts moving again. "Our goalie Isaac passes out when he's pooping."

"Stop it," Mara says.

"Yeah, he's hit his head on the way down before. One of our teammates dragged him out of the stall with his pants around his ankles and we had to make sure he was still alive."

"Defecation syncope," Aden says. "Straining

during bowel movements causes a drop in blood pressure for some people and they can pass out."

"How do you know that?" Harry asks.

"I was premed, but I dropped out."

"Right." Harry nods. "You told me that."

"I threw up on a nun once," Aden says.

There's a moment of silence and then Mara cackles. "We're going to need the full story on that one."

"I went to Catholic school, and I told Sister Agnes Marie I was going to be sick. She didn't believe me." He shrugs.

"I got caught pooping in the woods once," Suki blurts.

Carter gives her a look that's half-amused, half-impressed. "Who caught you?"

She rolls her eyes. "Some judgmental, middle-aged hag. My family had rented a cabin for the week, and there was only one bathroom. One of my brothers was in there one morning and I had to go. He wouldn't get out, so I went into the woods and did what I had to do. This couple on a walking trail saw me and the wife lectured me about burying poop in the woods."

Lainey looks tired, but her expression is relaxed. I hope she's realizing she's not alone. We don't all have IBS, but we can identify with her.

"I clogged the toilet at the office where I was doing a summer internship in high school," I say. "It was the front office of a minor league hockey team. I had to go ask the office manager, Linda, for a plunger."

Everyone laughs. Dex looks like he's trying to twerk while sitting. The whiskey is hitting.

The limo driver stops in front of Harry's house, a neat Craftsman style on the edge of the city.

"Great night, you guys. Thanks for everything," Harry says.

The girls all hug him and Aden, and the guys shake hands with them.

"Aden, come to our next fondue night!" Suki says.

"I'd love to."

When they get out of the car, the driver asks where we're going next.

Dex burps and laughs. "Mara, I think I need to stay with you tonight."

Mara gives the driver her address and he starts driving. I whisper in Lainey's ear, my arm still around her shoulders.

"How are you doing?"

"I'm good," she says softly. "You?"

"Great." I kiss the side of her head.

I'm maybe a foot from her breasts. They're basically milky round sirens calling out to me.

Touch us, Bash. Suck our nipples. Watch us bounce.

I force my gaze away. Not tonight. Lainey needs to chill.

Carter and Suki definitely won't be chilling. They're making out nearby, and he's right on the edge of pulling her into his lap.

"Let's order pizza and watch *Housewives*," Dex says to Mara.

"After I puke," she says.

I groan, wondering how much the limo company will charge me for puke cleanup. "Are you gonna puke?"

"Eh." Her shoulders slump. "When I get home."

"Maybe we should open the sunroof thing and you could stand up and get some air on your face," Dex suggests.

She shakes her head. "We'll be home soon. I can make it."

Lainey empties the contents of her purse onto the seat. "You can puke in here if you need to. I don't like this bag much anyway."

Mara smiles weakly. "Thanks. Whose idea was it to drink whiskey?"

She sips on water until we pull up in front of her apartment building ten minutes later.

"You need help getting in?" I ask her.

Dex jumps out of the car first. "Nah, I've got her. This ain't our first rodeo."

Mara doesn't get out of the car. It's more of a flow. She just bursts out of it, landing on her hands and knees and immediately puking on the sidewalk.

"I'm fine!" She puts a palm out. "Carry on. Thanks for a great night."

"You're such a professional," Suki calls out. "Love you! Go crawl in bed."

Dex gets her on her feet and they head for the front door of her building, her head slumped on his shoulder as he supports her weight with an arm around her back.

"You might be getting lucky tonight, Mr. Stanton," Suki tells Carter.

"I'm lucky every day I'm married to you."

"Aw, babe, you're making me reconsider swallowing."

Lainey is shaking with silent laughter next to me. I shake my head.

It's a relief to finally drop them off a few minutes later.

"Think they'll make it inside before they start going at it?" I ask Lainey.

"I'm like fifty-fifty on that."

She's so damn beautiful. Her eyes are the shade of emeralds and her smile is enough to turn a shitty day into a great one. I just look at her for a few seconds, knowing I want to see her face every day, whether she's laughing or crying. Furious or overjoyed.

"Tonight was perfect," she whispers. "Other than...you know, the gas station bathroom stop."

I cup her cheek. "It was perfect. I don't want a woman with a cast iron stomach. I want you."

She puts a hand on my knee. "I want you, too. I don't think I ever stopped wanting you."

"It's not happening tonight."

Her expression falls. "I think I could—"

"Nope. We're getting our pajamas on and watching TV in bed."

She bites her lower lip, and I wonder what she's thinking about. Waking up together? That's what I'm thinking about.

"There was a study that found people's eye blinking patterns synchronize with scene changes when they watch TV in bed. Isn't that crazy?"

A grin spreads across my face. "I love you, Lainey.

You're not like anyone else. There's only one perfect Delaney Morris in this world, and I'm so in love with you. I'm sorry it took me so long to chase after you the way you deserve."

A bright-pink flush covers her cheeks. "What if the sex is disappointing?"

I laugh heartily at that. "It won't be. I'm fully expecting you to stop me in the middle to tell me about a recent study done on sex hormones."

She laughs. "I could wait until after, unless I was bored out of my mind."

I slide an arm around her back and the other behind her knees, pulling her onto my lap. "You won't be."

She rests her forehead against mine, her lips an inch from my mouth as she speaks softly.

"I like that you're sweet and attentive. I love it. You made me feel special tonight. But when we're in bed, I want your primal side."

I was hard from the moment I put her on my lap, but now my balls tighten to an ache. She just ruined my plans to make love to her gently, and I'm fucking beside myself with excitement.

"You sure about that?" I squeeze her ass and she lets out a little moan. "You might get more than you bargained for."

Her exhale brushes across my lips, warm and sensual. "I've been reading dirty romance novels since I was fourteen. I don't want it soft and sweet. I want to be used by you. I want you to..." Her voice trails off and every muscle in my body tightens as I wait for her to continue.

"What? Tell me what you want, Lane. Please."

"I want you to tell me I'm a good girl while you're coming on me," she whispers. "Make me be dirty for you and then tell me how much you like it."

I groan and kiss her jawline, then her neck, murmuring against her skin. "You want to be my dirty girl?"

"Yes."

"No one else ever gets to see that side of you. That's only for me."

She gasps softly. "Yes. I've never told anyone else what I want."

I hold her close, my heart hammering against my rib cage. "I want to know all of it. And I want to give you anything you want from me. Of me. I never want you to look at another man and wish for anything."

She sinks her nails into my shoulder as I kiss her neck. "Will I be the only woman you wish for, though?"

"You already are," I say softly in her ear. "You know me in ways no one else does. You love me for who I am, even though I'm not as brilliant and funny as you are."

She hums as the car slows to a stop. "Yes, you are. And I do love you, Bash. So much."

We're at my house. That has to be why the car isn't moving. But I don't want to get out. I've never had such an intimate exchange with anyone, and I don't want it to end.

She moves off my lap, packing her things back into her purse.

I help, passing her a pack of gum and a lipstick. "That was nice of you to offer Mara your bag to puke in."

"I'm glad she didn't need it."

We get out of the car and I walk over to the driver, passing him a cash tip. "Thanks, man."

"Thank you, sir." He waves and drives away. Lainey and I walk to my garage door keypad.

"A shower and pajamas sounds nice," she says.

"Wear the ones with cats in cowboy hats."

She laughs. "Those aren't sexy at all. Don't you want to know what you're missing?"

I kiss her. "They're sexy on you. And good things come to those who wait."

She leads the way into the house, my gaze locked onto her ass. The things I'm going to do to that ass. I want her body so badly I'm practically shaking,

Soon. Very soon.

CHAPTER TWENTY

Lainey

I OPEN MY EYES, surprised when it's not Bash's guest room I see.

His bedroom has simple white walls with no decor. A framed black-and-white photo of his parents sits on his dresser beside another one of Kramer, his childhood dog.

I used to peek through my bedroom blinds to see him when he walked Kramer, a beagle. Every evening, they'd go by, Kramer's nose to the ground and his tail wagging.

His king-size bed is firm and comfortable. I fell

asleep so quickly after I took a shower and put on the pajamas he requested.

"Hey, good morning."

His morning voice is even deeper than his usual one, and it sends a delicious shiver down my spine. He's lying next to me, shirtless, looking at his phone.

"Good morning."

He sets his phone down and turns onto his side, facing me. "How'd you sleep?"

"So good. You?"

"Great." He brushes a strand of hair away from my face. "Since we're both off today, I was thinking we could have our second date."

Warmth fills my chest. "Were you? What did you have in mind?"

"Thought we could go out for breakfast, maybe do some shopping. Have you ever been to the West Side Market?"

"No."

"It's nice. Lots of produce and fresh meat and fish. We could get something to make for dinner tonight."

My gaze slides from the shadow of scruff on his cheeks down to his chest. I've seen it before—muscles for days and dark hair—but there's something about seeing it when he's beside me in bed that's next level.

"I'm down for all of the above, but I'd like to make an addition."

"What's that?" he asks.

"Morning sex."

His lips part, quirking at the corners. "Yeah?"

"Yeah."

He comes closer, about to kiss me, when I put my hand over his mouth. "First, we have to both brush our teeth. I know too much about the science of morning breath—sorry."

His laugh tickles over my fingers. "You're good. I'll go get a root canal right now if that's what it takes."

He's out of bed and in the bathroom in about three seconds flat. I bite my lip because even though he was practically sprinting, I still got to enjoy the view of him in nothing but boxers.

I've never dreamed I'd have all six feet, two inches and two hundred twenty pounds of Sebastian Stone focused entirely on me in bed. I'm nervous but mostly excited. I'm not letting IBS ruin this for me again.

When I get to the bathroom, Bash is inside the

separate toilet room, peeing. I hurry into my bathroom upstairs and pee, brush my teeth and swish around some mouthwash.

I give myself a little high five in the mirror and then go back downstairs, checking off boxes in my head.

Legs: shaved. Pits: also shaved. Vag: kinda trimmed. Breath: good.

When I get back into the bedroom, Bash is lying there on his side, his erection tenting his boxers.

I suck in a breath, wishing I could take a picture of him right now. But why look at a picture when I have the real thing? He's warm and hard and waiting *for me.*

"Get over here right now."

His command makes excitement swirl in my stomach. I take a step forward, then stop, reaching for the first button on my pajama shirt. When I unfasten it, Bash's eyes widen.

"Fuck yes, baby. Strip for me."

He gets to his knees on the bed, his erection infusing me with confidence. I move a little closer—slowly—and keep unbuttoning my shirt. Once it's all the way open, I stand at the foot of the bed and open it for him, sliding it off my shoulders and letting it drop to the floor.

"So beautiful," he breathes, mesmerized.

I take a step back and slide my sleep shorts down, my underwear going down, too. Bash's lips part and he scrambles out of his boxers like his life depends on it.

I've never felt so powerful. He's on his knees for me in every way right now.

"Remember what I said I wanted," I say softly.

"Yes. But I love you, Lane. Whatever I say in this bed, I want you to know up front that I fucking love you so much I can hardly breathe."

I nod, my heart bursting with happiness. "I love you, too, Bash. And I'm on birth control. So as long as you don't have—"

"I don't. I get tested every four weeks by the team doctor."

He gets out of bed, putting his hands on my waist. His gaze is wolfish, making me feel like prey. I love it.

"Good girls don't tease. Are you teasing me, Delaney?"

"No." My core clenches with arousal. "Yes. Am I?"

"Yes."

He weighs one of my breasts in his hand, his thumb brushing over my nipple. "You want these sucked, don't you?"

"Yes." It's not just my face but my whole body that flushes.

His gaze tracks down. "That orange hair on your cunt is sexy as fuck. Don't ever shave it."

Oh God. I'm dead. Bash just killed me by saying the word *cunt*.

He brushes his thumb over my curls, lightly running the tip of his thumb down my slit. I look away, overwhelmed by sensation, but he tips my chin back up so we're eye to eye.

"I'm gonna fill this sweet cunt up. Stretch it out and fuck it hard."

I moan softly.

"But first, you're gonna get on your knees for me."

He wraps a hand around his cock, his order coming out in a rasp. I drop to the floor on my knees, my nipples pebbled. This is more incredible than any fantasy I've ever had.

The corners of his lips tilt up as he rakes his fingers into my hair, guiding my head toward his large, thick erection. When I slide my lips over his head, he groans.

"Such a good girl. You're a hungry little whore, aren't you?"

I hum my enthusiastic agreement.

"Hungry for my cock. Desperate for my cum."

I take as much of him as I can, my hand wrapped around the base of his cock. After about a minute, he pulls back, reaching down to help me up.

He gets in bed, stretching out on his back. His heated gaze rakes up and down my body.

"Ride my cock. I want to watch you get your little cunt off. I want the sweet, innocent woman I love to show me what a dirty little slut she really is."

"Bash, I've never...done that." I tuck my hair behind my ear, self-conscious.

"Even better. Come on, I know you want it."

I do. I really, really do, but I don't want to mess it up. I walk over to the side of the bed and put a knee on it. Bash, propped up on his elbows, nods toward his gleaming erection, pointing straight up at the ceiling.

"Don't make me wait. I want that tight little pussy wrapped around my cock."

His mouth is even sexier than the rest of him. I'm so turned on, and obviously, he is, too.

Fuck it. He'll help me if I mess up. I straddle him, a satisfied groan leaving his lips as he lines himself up at my entrance. His groan intensifies as I sink down onto him.

He's much bigger than I've had before. I get about

halfway down his length before I pull back up, my eyes finding his.

"So fucking good." His hands are wrapped around my waist, supporting me.

When I move again, going a little farther this time, he makes a strangled noise. I don't know if it's possible to mess this up. He seems to be loving it, and I love the full feeling of him inside me.

"Lean forward," he says. "Put your hands on my shoulders."

I do, crying out when I sink even farther onto him. It's a full feeling, but it doesn't hurt. It actually feels amazing.

He guides my hips up and down, and I quickly see why he told me to move. In this position, my clit is rubbing up and down his cock with every thrust.

"Oh...I like that," I breathe. "Keep doing that."

It's not just me fucking him—he's thrusting up into me, his hold on my waist keeping me steady. This isn't just good—it's amazing. I've always been a passive participant in sex, but this time I'm doing what's good for me.

I reach for the headboard, wrapping one hand around the top of it. It positions me perfectly, and I moan every time he's all the way inside me because it's everything. We're moving faster now, arousal swelling hard and fast inside me.

"I'm gonna fill your cunt up." His voice is strained. "I'm gonna come inside you so hard."

His words and the way he pinches my nipple tip me over the edge. I ride him with abandon, crying out his name and every swear word I know as I reach a blissful peak and ride it out.

I'm coming down, breathless, when he grips my waist tighter and thrusts up into me twice, holding himself deep inside as he groans hard and finds his release.

"Holy fuck." He lets go of me and drops his head back to the bed. "I might've just blown a hole through your back."

I slide off him and curl up beside him, limp with satisfaction. "Worth it."

He tilts my chin up for a soft, slow kiss. "You're incredible."

"Thanks for finally realizing it," I crack.

He kisses me again. "If I'm being honest, the first time I felt an attraction to you was at your twenty-first birthday party."

Eric rented out a local bar for the occasion, and I remember that Bash was there, but I don't recall seeing much of him.

"Really?"

"Yeah. You looked really curvy and sexy in that denim dress."

I consider. "I did gain fifteen pounds my sophomore year of college."

"I hadn't seen you in a while, and you looked damn good. But I didn't make a move because you were in college and...it just wouldn't have worked."

"And then I started dating he who shall not be named."

He moves his hand to my breast, cupping it. "If you'd gone through with the wedding, I would have responded when they asked if anyone objected until I got dragged out of the church. Then I would've busted out a window and kept objecting."

"Really?"

"I'm used to fighting for what I want."

I kiss him, imagining myself falling into his arms while wearing a wedding dress. It's...nice. Really nice.

"So now you want to get ready and go out for the day?" I ask.

He sighs heavily. "I did suggest that, didn't I?"

"We could always go out later. For lunch?"

A smile plays on his lips. "Dinner. I'll make us

some lunch later. And don't worry, I'll carry you to dinner."

I frown. "Why would I need that?"

"Because you won't be able to walk."

I smile, my girly parts already tingling with anticipation. "We'll see about that, Mr. Stone. It would take a lot of fucking for that to happen."

"That's exactly what I have planned."

CHAPTER TWENTY-ONE

Bash

A BUMPY PLANE landing wakes me from a deep sleep. I wipe the drool away from my mouth and sit up.

We left Vancouver late last night and we're arriving in Tampa now. The regular season has started with a bang. We left Cleveland a few days ago for a six-day stretch of travel. With the crazy travel hours, we have to just catch sleep when we can and make do with what we get.

We're 3–0, though, so no one's complaining.

Missing Lainey is a lot harder on me than the travel. We got three nights together before I left, and we made the most of them.

I wasn't her first, but there was so much she'd never experienced before me. Shitty Shane never gave her oral. He never tried ass play or fingering her. From what she's said, he's as boring and vanilla as I would've guessed.

Fine by me. It's incredible seeing her experience things for the first time. She's adventurous, with encouragement. Every time we're together, her confidence grows.

Though I didn't even realize it was happening, I found the one. I don't want anyone else, and I don't like being away from Lainey. There's no way around it when I'm traveling for hockey, but that's not what I'm most concerned about.

I can't stop thinking about the letter I sorted out of the pile of mail for her. The return address was in Israel. It has to be from the place that's one of her top two choices for her next research position.

Just the thought of her going back to Columbus at the end of the semester is hard; I can't even imagine her going to another fucking country.

Leo scowls at me as the interior lights of the plane are turned on.

"The fuck? Where are we?"

"Tampa."

"Shit." He rubs his face. "Feels like we took off five minutes ago."

"We get to sleep for a few hours at our hotel," I remind him.

"Good. I'm a zombie."

It's dark and humid out as we all file off the plane and walk to the bus that's taking us to our hotel. My teammate Andrei has a newborn at home, so he doesn't even sleep much there. He curled up in the corner of our locker room and took a nap yesterday.

I love this game. Even the demanding travel schedule. If it was easy, everyone would do it. The work and discipline it takes to hang with these guys is part of the reason I love and respect them so much.

But I'm turning twenty-nine next month, and I'm starting to think about having more than hockey in my life. I've been doing this for eleven years, and I've got a few more in me.

Then what, though? I've always known I wanted kids, and I'm not sure how Lainey feels about that. She's worked hard to get where she is, and all the dreams she talks about are professional.

Does she want a family? She's only twenty-four, so I get why she might not be thinking about it yet.

It's frustrating as hell, respecting what she does,

but wondering if that's her only priority. Sort of like being with a pro hockey player; we can have relationships and get married, but our partners have to respect that we don't get to choose where we live. We travel eight months a year—if we're in the play-offs—and we could get traded and have to upend our lives.

How do we make a relationship work when her career will be like that, too? I don't like thinking about it. We're still in that brand-new honeymoon phase, where everything is amazing and arguments don't exist. I want to stay there, but Lainey's only scheduled to be in Cleveland for two more months.

Two fucking months. Is that long enough to convince her to stay? I already know I want that. I want her Pop-Tart crumbs on my counter and her satin underwear on my bathroom floor. I want her in my bed. At my kitchen table. In the stands at my games. With me and my friends.

She has to want that, too, though. It's too soon to buy a ring but damn if a big part of me isn't ready.

When we get to our hotel, we all wait in the lobby with our bags as an assistant coach checks us in. It's taking forever. Leo is already asleep on a lobby couch.

"Guys, I've got bad news," Coach Turner says.

We all gather around to hear what he's saying.

"There's a problem. Firefighters have been fighting a massive fire here, and some of them needed to rest, so the hotel apparently left a message on someone's voicemail in the front office that we're getting seventeen rooms instead of thirty-five."

Someone sighs heavily.

"No problem, Coach," Carter says. "Tell 'em we'll give up more rooms if the firefighters need them. We can double up in the beds."

Everyone nods and murmurs their agreement. We're tired, but it's nothing compared to what firefighters do.

"Let's buy them a meal," Isaac says. "All the firefighters. Can someone from the team set that up?"

Our general manager, Marie Mathias, who's traveling with us on this trip, answers.

"Absolutely. The team will take care of the arrangements and we'll cover the cost."

"What else can we do?" I ask.

"I'll look into it," Marie says. "Our game tomorrow night is still on as of now, but that could change depending on this fire."

"For now, sleep," Coach says. "Andy is working

on room assignments. If you complain about your roommate, you'll be sleeping on the bus."

I'm paired with Andrei. We have to share a king bed, but he's curled up on one side with his back to me, snoring before I even get my shoes off.

I'm tired, too. I had to watch video of my shifts from our last game on the flight, and I was only able to sleep for about the last twenty minutes of it.

And we'll do it all again in a few hours—if the game doesn't get canceled.

I plug my phone charger in and lie down, rereading the text Lainey sent me last night. There's a photo of her and Bruce snuggling in my bed.

Lainey: We miss you! Good luck! Text me when you land. xoxo

She's makeup-free in the photo, her hair damp from a shower. Her pajamas are covered in bananas wearing glasses and reading books.

I wish it was her beside me instead of Andrei.

I text her.

Bash: I miss you too. More than you know. We're in Tampa and I'm about to get some sleep. Can't wait to see you.

Turning my phone face down on the nightstand, I close my eyes, hoping I can sleep. My mind is preoccupied with thoughts of Lainey and the future.

Sleep doesn't come easily. Now that I know what it's like to be with her, I don't know how I could ever go back to the way it was before.

CHAPTER TWENTY-TWO

Lainey

"Where's Uncle Bashie?"

Ugh, my aching ovaries. I'd forgotten that my niece Avana calls Bash that. She's in Cleveland with Eric and Callie for the weekend, and we're all at Bash's game against St. Louis at his home arena.

"He'll be out there, punk." I pick Avana up and point out to the ice. "We're going to watch him play hockey."

Her whole face lights up as she points to the ice. "Uncle Bashie!"

"Yes, baby. Soon." I kiss the top of her head.

We're in a suite an usher brought us to, where the

Crush family members gather for a buffet and social hour before the game. I smile as Suki brings Charlotte and Hallie over.

"Hey, girl." She gives me a half hug since I'm holding Avana. "Who's this cutie?"

"This is my niece, Avana. And this is my brother Eric and my sister-in-law Callie."

"Eric and Callie!" Suki lights up. "Bash and Lainey have told us all about you."

Eric frowns. "All lies."

She laughs. "It was all good, promise. I'm so glad you guys are here. Have you eaten?"

"I'm not sure there's enough food," Callie deadpans.

The buffet is an absolute feast, with long tables loaded with wings, burgers, soup, salad, potato skins, mac and cheese, roasted vegetables, and several desserts.

"Are you hungry?" I ask Avana.

She shakes her head, wiggling to get out of my hold.

"I should probably take her to the bathroom," Callie says.

"I'll take her," I say. "You guys eat."

"Great, thanks."

I hold Avana's hand and lead her out of the suite.

People I don't even know smile and nod at me when we walk out. Everyone here is friendly, easing my nerves about attending my first game as Bash's girlfriend.

There are TV screens hanging on walls and mounted in corners, all broadcasting pregame coverage. I pause when I see a shot of the crowd entering the arena, the back of one of the jerseys showing Bash's name and number.

He has fans. I knew that, but being here is really making it sink in. I'm not just with a hockey player; I'm with a hockey star. People enthusiastically spend their time and money to come watch the Crush play.

That has to be high pressure for the players. I imagine doing my research in the center of an arena, tens of thousands of people watching and cheering for me to succeed.

Damn. It has to feel terrible to disappoint people, even when the players know they gave it their all. Bash told me he has a game-day routine and that he might seem emotionally unavailable on those days unless I have an emergency.

I'm realizing what that means. When he was traveling, we exchanged minimal texts. Mostly just checking in to say hey when he arrived in a new city. I actually liked it because, on those days, I could throw myself into work at the lab and spend time alone at home.

I need my alone time. Suki and Mara are extroverts; they seem to thrive when they're with their people. And I love that, too, but I also need time to recharge my social battery.

Silence is golden sometimes. I like to bake bread, read, or rot in front of the TV all alone sometimes. It makes my time with Bash feel more special.

"Where's Uncle Bashie?" Avana scans the arena hallways for him.

"You'll see him soon. He'll be out on the ice playing hockey."

We use the bathroom, which is an adventure. I have to go, too, which means keeping her in the stall with me. I have a new appreciation for Callie as I pee while trying to keep Avana from touching anything.

"Mommy says hold hands," she tells me, taking both of my hands in hers.

Genius. Callie must have her daughter hold hands with her while she pees to keep her from picking up ten thousand germs and microbes.

I have to wipe, but I can do that one-handed.

When I'm helping her wash her hands, I smooth a hand over my niece's little blond ponytail. She's wearing a little version of the same sweater I have on, which is Bash's. I really wanted to wear one of his, and he told me to take anything I wanted from his closet, but they were just too big. They all hung past my fingertips and looked ridiculous on me. So I went with a smaller one he got me from a merch stand at the arena.

Once back in the suite, Avana and I eat. I'm careful to stick to low-fat foods. Avana has three bites of mac and cheese and that's it. Hallie is leading her around the suite, enjoying her opportunity to be the bigger kid for once.

"So you and Bash." Callie gives me a giddy smile. "I'm so happy for you."

I get warm all over, grinning. "Thanks. It's...I mean, he's amazing. Really. He sent me flowers today."

She puts a hand on her chest. "How sweet. Roses?"

"Two dozen purple roses. My favorite color."

She looks at my brother and clears her throat dramatically. "Are you taking notes, Eric?"

He gives her a wry look. "Yeah, I'm all over it."

That floral delivery made me cry. I was so surprised. It was my first time getting flowers, and when I read the card, I lost it.

. . .

LAINEY, today is one of many firsts for us. I love you. - Bash

I NEVER WANT TO LEAVE. Though I'm doing what I have to do and looking into my options for next semester, there's a sense of dread when I do.

The place in Israel sent me information to apply. I emailed about Cambridge and they don't have openings but they put me on a waiting list.

It's time to decide where I'm going next semester and also next year if I want to become a full-time student working on my doctorate.

I'm torn. I love the research I'm finally getting to focus on. I worked hard on my bachelor's and then my master's, and this is the payoff. A doctorate would open more doors for me, but I'm really enjoying the doors that are open right now.

And Bash. For the first time in my life, my greatest joy isn't coming from academic or professional accomplishments. I would have liked to date in high school, but it wasn't in the cards for me. So, instead, I threw myself into my classes, graduating as one of seven valedictorians.

I don't love Bash because he's a star hockey player. I loved him long before that. And he sees through my accomplishments to me and loves me for who I am, not what I've done.

I've seen other women be loved like this. But me? I never expected it to happen. This isn't a fling. I'm not scratching an itch. What I have with Bash fills a part of me I didn't even realize was empty before.

"Shane saw the picture of you and Bash that Bash posted on his socials." Callie looks smug. "I asked Brielle to ask one of the guys he games with. Shane said you cheated on him with Bash and that's why you guys broke up."

"Bull. Shit."

"I know. But the point is, he saw it. He knows."

I don't have strong feelings about that. I guess I'm glad he knows I moved on, but I don't wish bad things for Shane. His indifference and carelessness saved me from a disappointing marriage, so it's hard to resent him.

Eric shakes his head. "He's a tool. I'm really glad I don't have to pretend I'm interested in him telling me about pool maintenance. Why the hell would I care? I don't have a pool, and I don't plan to get one."

I laugh, remembering all the times I had to feign interest in pool chemical balances.

"It's like me talking to someone in a casual conversation and being like, 'Hey, do you know about insurance subrogation?'" Eric continues. "I'm just going to drone about it until you fall asleep."

"I wish you'd told me how you really felt about him," I say.

"I do, too. I gave Bash so much crap for complaining about him, and..." He shrugs. "He was right."

"Yeah, but let's not remind him of that," I quip. "His ego is big enough."

"Lainey!"

A woman wraps her arms around my neck from behind. I turn my neck to find Mara, who kisses me on the cheek.

"Wait a minute." Eric gives me a shocked look. "You have *two* friends here?"

I roll my eyes at him. "Yes, I do, and they're nicer to me than my own family."

Mara stands. "She's got four friends here, and we're not sharing her with anyone else. This girl's a trivia goddess."

"You seem to be feeling better than the last time I saw you," I say, smiling.

"Oh yeah. Dex and I had a very slow day after that night."

We missed our last trivia night because Mara was tied up at work. She recently started a new job in the state's attorney's office, and they had a backlog of cases.

"I'm Mara Diaz," she says, extending a hand to Eric.

"Sorry," I say. "Mara, this is my brother Eric and my sister-in-law Callie. My niece Avana is here somewhere. She's with Hallie."

"It's great to meet you." Mara looks at me. "You guys are coming to the Halloween party, right?"

"Wouldn't miss it."

She gives me a quick hug. "I'm going to stuff my face. I'll see you later."

"Be good. I'll see you soon." I check my watch. "The pregame show is starting soon. We should get to our seats."

Bash got us seats on the glass for Avana's first hockey game. He didn't get them from the team because the tickets he forwarded to my phone were from a ticketing app and I saw how much he paid for them. Let's just say he's a really nice boyfriend, uncle, brother, and brother-in-law.

"Uncle Bashie!" Avana leans forward, a hand on the glass, when the pregame light and video show ends and Bash skates out with the rest of his team.

He gives her a little wave, then shoots me a wink.

Callie leans over and speaks in my ear. "You're

going to have his babies. I know it. I can't even stand how happy I am for you."

A thrill of excitement shoots to my stomach. Bash asked me casually the other day if I wanted kids. When I told him I did, he smiled and said he did, too.

I'm still afraid to dream that dream. Just having Bash see me the way I always longed for him to see me, hearing him tell me he loves me, and getting flowers from him is everything.

I love it all. His voice, his smile, his arms around me. The sweetness only I get to see, and the sexy, commanding man that's also only for me.

If I wasn't already waist-deep in researching the human microbiome, I'd study the love hormones like serotonin, norepinephrine, and dopamine. Vasopressin is particularly fascinating. It helps the human body conserve water and regulates sodium levels, but it's also part of people—especially men— forming long-term emotional attachments and protective behaviors.

I've read about these things and thought of them in clinical terms, but now I get to *feel* them.

Bash gets checked into the boards by a St. Louis player. He recovers quickly and gets back to playing, seeming unfazed.

"These seats are unreal," Eric says. "I can see their sweat."

It is pretty incredible to be so close to the action. The man who gently stroked a hand over my hair and kissed me on the forehead before leaving home early this morning drives his shoulder into an opponent, knocking him off balance.

Bash quickly regains control of the puck and shoots it into the net. The arena erupts, horns blaring and people cheering. Alana claps, oblivious to the chaos with her noise-canceling headphones on.

The goal Bash scored ends up being the only one in the game, and the mood in the room we sit in to wait for him after the game is high. Alana was exhausted by the third period, so Callie took her back to Bash's to go to bed and now it's just Eric and I waiting.

When he walks into the room in a dark suit with a white shirt and a light-blue tie, Bash's gaze goes right to me. I stand up, my heart racing with excitement.

He's wearing the hell out of that suit. His hair is still damp from the shower and I take in his familiar amber-and-pine scent as he hugs me and kisses me.

It's a soft, chaste kiss, probably because my brother is two feet away.

"Great game," I murmur in his ear.

"Thanks."

He grins at Eric and shakes his hand. "You made it."

"Wouldn't miss it. Hell of a game, man."

The others are going out, but we're going home. We're getting up early tomorrow, so we stay aligned with Avana's sleep schedule. And we're going to take Eric and his family to a few of our favorite Cleveland places.

This city is quickly starting to feel like home to me. Or maybe that's just Bash that feels like home. Either way, if he wants me to stay when my semester is over, I'm in.

I can do research from anywhere. Maybe not as part of a large team, but that's okay. There's only one Sebastian Stone, and now that he's finally mine, I go where he goes.

Bash

"Seriously, there should be a hole in that suit." I rake my gaze up and down Lainey's body in her costume. "Like long underwear. An access flap I can open to fuck you and then close again so we can mingle at this party."

She rolls her eyes, feigning aggravation. Because honestly, she loves *too horny to live* Bash and we both know it. She's pure smoke in her Catwoman suit, and even though we spent an hour in bed earlier this afternoon, I want her again already.

"It's the ears, isn't it?" She makes a kissy face, teasing me.

"Yeah, I'm sure that's it," I say dryly.

Her tits look incredible in the outfit, even though her chest is completely covered. I probably should have put her in a frumpy Robin outfit instead of getting us these expensive custom-made Batman and Catwoman costumes because every guy who sees her tonight is going to have his tongue on the floor.

When she puts on the mask and holds the whip that came with the costume, Lainey looks like a high-dollar dominatrix. Her bright-red hair, flowing around her shoulders, only adds to her appeal. Normally I'm in charge in our bedroom, but for a change of pace, I'd lick her shiny black boots and take orders.

"We're so much smarter than Carter and Suki." I grin. "They're bacon and eggs. Those costumes will be useless in their bedroom tonight."

"It's cute, though."

My dog sitter River comes into the kitchen from the backyard, Bruce on his heels.

"Hey, you guys look awesome," he says.

River has long, scraggly blond hair and he doesn't shave much, so his beard comes down to his chest. He's wearing a tie-dye T-shirt and he's definitely stoned. His skin is bronzed from his summer back-packing in Patagonia.

Living in my guest cottage for eight months a year during hockey season to take care of Bruce when I'm traveling is River's main job. It works well because he takes great care of him, and he's able to travel during my offseason.

"That sourdough is ready to eat. Help yourself," Lainey says.

River grins. "Amazing. Thank you."

She's been keeping him supplied with bread and muffins, and he loves it. Lainey reminds me of Suki in many ways—she loves caring for people. My kitchen is finally being used by someone other than my chef. Lainey loves my oven, and I love seeing her wearing an apron. One of these days, she's going to give in to my requests that she wear an apron and nothing else while she's baking. I fantasize when I'm traveling about bending her over the island and holding onto the bow at her back while I ravage her.

Not while River's here, though. Hell, I probably won't even let Bruce be around for it. No one wants to watch their mom get plowed.

"I'm gonna make a veggie sandwich with that bread and then Bruce and I are going to have massage time," River says.

I groan. "You're gonna massage his prostate again, aren't you?"

Laney gapes at me but says nothing. River just grins.

"Yeah, man. Full body. He's not getting his rocks off; it's to improve blood flow to his prostate."

I look at Bruce, who cocks his head. "Right, but I'm never going near his prostate. You walk him three times a day, feed him a raw diet, take him on hikes, and rub his prostate. Which, let's be honest— he probably enjoys it. He probably wishes you were his real dad."

River and Lainey both laugh, but this really is one of my fears.

"He's actually not a big fan of having his bung-hole penetrated. It took us time to build up the trust for it. And he hates it when I brush his teeth and make him take his vitamins."

I sigh heavily. "Just don't get my dog off, okay? Please?"

"No worries, brother. I'm just here to holistically help his body and spirit."

I don't even know how to respond to that. Thankfully, Lainey saves me from having to.

"Hey, we need to go," she says.

We both pet Bruce before leaving, and he still wags his tail and licks my face, so he must still love me. This must be what it feels like for parents to leave their kids with a nanny.

I glance over at Lainey's beat-up old Camry as I back my truck out of the garage, thinking about the Christmas gift I just ordered for her.

It's a brand-new BMW X5, and I ordered it early because it's getting a custom dark-purple paint job. It's so dark it's almost black, and the interior is black leather. I know she's going to flip.

If I'd asked her if I could buy her a new car, she would have refused. This way, it'll already be here and she can't say no.

Lainey deserves every luxury. Once we had *the talk*, and I asked her to stay with me after this semester if at all possible, she decided to start working on her doctorate. She found a program through Cleveland Clinic where she could work on her doctorate part-time while also researching. Helping Professor Carr with his classes has sparked a love of teaching in her.

For the first time, I'm hoping I don't make the all-star team. I'm not expecting to because Isaac and Carter are having once-in-a-lifetime seasons this year. If I don't, Lainey and I are taking a six-day trip to Fiji. Six days and nights of nothing but the two of us would be paradise no matter where we were, but we'll still make the most of our time in a little hut built over sparkling turquoise water.

I'm planning to propose on the trip. It's soon, but also not soon enough. Being with Lainey feels like an unlocking of sorts. All the clicks and slides fell into place and something inside me opened for the first time. I never knew what people meant when they said, "When you know, you know." Until I knew. Then I got it.

This is what it means to feel complete. I don't have any doubts. Lainey is my one and only.

When we arrive at Carter and Suki's house, the front yard has been decorated with lights, smoke machines and animatronic monsters. There's even Halloween music playing in the front yard.

Inside, the lights are dimmed and every room on the main level is decorated. There are fake spiderwebs and bats hanging from the ceiling and fake skeletons wearing hockey gear in corners.

A coffin in the dining room is open, the inside filled with an assortment of snacks. There's a fake head in the center of the dining table, its eyes following me wherever I move.

A guy dressed as a vampire comes up to us with a tray of drinks. It takes us a few seconds to figure out that it's Aden, Harry's boyfriend.

"Hey, man. Good to see you again," I say.

"Would you like some fresh blood?" he offers, gesturing to his tray.

"Yum." Lainey grabs a glass and takes a sip, looking at me. "Red wine."

"Love your costumes," Aden says.

"Yours, too," Lainey says. "Is Harry here?"

"He got called to the restaurant for an emergency. He wasn't happy. There was a water main break, though. Pretty big deal."

"Oh, damn," I say. "They'll have to close."

"Do I look horny, baby?" A huge man approaches us from behind, putting an arm around Bash's shoulders and the other around mine.

His British accent is terrible, but Leo's costume is on point. He's Austin Powers, complete with a dark wig, glasses and bell-bottom pants.

Bash laughs heartily as he takes in Leo's outfit.

"'Bout time you bought a costume," Leo says, nodding at Bash's Batsuit. "And *damn*, Lainey."

"That's enough looking at her," I gripe.

"You better keep her happy, or someone else will." Leo winks at her.

"Batman and Catwoman!"

Suki approaches us, Carter right beside her. She's dressed as a long, sizzling piece of bacon, her face poking out through an oval. Carter is a huge, round, fried egg, and he doesn't look thrilled about it.

"I keep running into doorframes," he grumbles.

It's Darling who steals the show, though. He's dressed as a bunny, with a soft gray covering on his body and a bunny ear headband Velcroed around his head. He wags his tail and smiles up at us, taking the cracker Leo offers him.

"I can't stand how cute he is," Mara says as she walks up.

"Oh my God, you look amazing!" Lainey says.

Mara is dressed as the Evil Queen from *Snow White*, and she makes a damn good one with her fair skin and black hair.

"Did you guys not tell Mara it's a costume party?" Leo asks.

"Hilarious," Mara deadpans. "I could say the same for you. Isn't horny perv your everyday look?"

"Hey, if you need to pick up some extra money, my neighbors are looking for some privacy hedges. You can go stand on their property line and open your legs."

Carter starts to laugh, then covers it with a cough and his hand.

"You thought of that one months ago, didn't you?" Mara says. "Been saving it up? Practicing it in front of the mirror?"

"Hey, at least I have mirrors in my house. Wouldn't you turn to stone if you looked in one?"

"Okay, this is fun," Suki interjects. "But we should probably mingle. All of us."

"Have they ever gotten along?" Lainey asks me softly when we are out of everyone else's hearing range.

"For a little while. She's never getting over him walking into that bathroom on her."

Lainey raises a shoulder. "Well, he was way out of line. And instead of apologizing, he made fun of her."

I pinch my brows together, remembering Leo's description of what happened between them. "Actually, she made fun of him first."

"Still. She gets a free pass. He should have apologized and closed the door immediately."

"Yeah."

She gives me a warning look. "You better knock on doors before opening them. Don't barge in on naked women."

I grin at her. "In Leo's defense, he did knock. But there was music playing and Mara must not have heard it. And I promise to knock loudly on every closed door for the rest of my life."

"Thank you."

I move to stand behind her, wrapping my arms around her waist. She laughs lightly.

"Is that your costume's codpiece, or are you just happy to see me?" she cracks.

I look down at her face. "My *what?*"

"Your codpiece. The part of your costume that covers your junk. I've been practicing trivia and that was one of my questions the other day."

I hum in amusement. "It should be called a cock-piece. And I am happy to see you. Ready to sneak off and explore your Catcave anytime."

She groans. "I can't decide if that's just gross or mostly gross with a slight twinge of hot."

"You liked it."

"I might've."

I spin her around so she's facing me, then take her masked face in my hands.

"It's our first Halloween together. This will probably be easier than our first Thanksgiving together."

Our mothers are already both insisting we spend the holiday with them. We're going to have to spend time at both houses and eat ourselves sick, so neither mom has hurt feelings.

"Probably," she agrees. "I'm still looking forward to it, though."

"Me too." I kiss her gently. "I'm looking forward to everything with you."

AUTHOR'S NOTE

Thanks for reading Wanting the Winger. Up next in this series is Getting the Grinder. It's the story of Leo and Mara. Is this going to be the most fun book I've ever written? I mean, it might be.

Book 2 - In Deep

Book 3 - Drawn Deeper

Book 4 - Hidden Depth

FILTHY SERIES

Book 1 - Dirty Work

Book 2 - Dirty Secret

Book 3 - Dirty Defiance

STANDALONES

Come Closer

Buried

Sweet Sixteen

His

Alpha Mail

Healing Touch

Barely Breathing

Exiled

Unspoken

ABOUT THE AUTHOR

Brenda Rothert lives in Central Illinois with her husband, children and three dogs. She loves to hear from readers through her website or her Facebook Group, Rothert's Readers.

Keep up with all the latest on Brenda's books and get bonus content by signing up for her newsletter HERE.